He slid his hands to her elbows, stopping her. "I'm not treating our first time together like we're teenagers looking for a fast thrill in a game room. We're not only too old for that, we deserve better."

Dusting her hands as if she was done, she hurried away. "Fine. This is all I have, Bryce. All I can do."

He touched her shoulder and she stopped. Did she want him to change her mind? Show her how much he cared about her? "If it were me... If our positions were reversed, and I was the one with scars, what would you do right now, Kylie? Would you let me run away? Continue to be afraid?"

She covered her face. "I am afraid."

He could barely hear her. He asked just as quietly, "Of me?"

"Strangely enough, no. But yes, maybe of you most of all."

GUNSLINGER

ANGI MORGAN

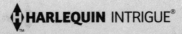

HARLEQUIN INTRIGUE®

There is never a book completed without my pals Jan and Robin.
This one also goes to my wonderful agent, Jill,
and to the patience of my amazing editor, Allison!
Thanks, ladies, for hanging in there with me.

ISBN-13: 978-0-373-74969-0

Gunslinger

Copyright © 2016 by Angela Platt

Recycling programs
for this product may
not exist in your area.

Printed in U.S.A.

www.Harlequin.com

Angi Morgan writes Harlequin Intrigue novels "where honor and danger collide with love." She combines actual Texas settings with characters who are in realistic and dangerous situations. Angi's work has been a finalist for numerous awards, including the Booksellers' Best Award and the Daphne du Maurier Award. Angi and her husband live in north Texas. Visit her website, angimorgan.com, or follow her on Facebook at Angi Morgan Books. She loves to hang out with fans in her closed group: bit.ly/angifriends.

Books by Angi Morgan

Harlequin Intrigue

Texas Rangers: Elite Troop

Bulletproof Badge
Shotgun Justice
Gunslinger

West Texas Watchmen

The Sheriff
The Cattleman
The Ranger

Texas Family Reckoning

Navy SEAL Surrender
The Renegade Rancher

Hill Country Holdup
.38 Caliber Cover-Up
Dangerous Memories
Protecting Their Child
The Marine's Last Defense

CAST OF CHARACTERS

Bryce Johnson—Lieutenant in the Texas Rangers and Company F's authority on Texas organized crime. He's on his first field assignment with a lot to prove. He can't afford to be wrong.

Kylie Scott—Media-shy resident who organizes youth to volunteer for the senior citizens of Hico. Does she have something or someone to hide from?

Sissy Jorgenson—Teenage supermodel who was briefly married to Xander Tenoreno. She disappeared from the hospital after her divorce and an attempt on her life.

Xander Tenoreno—A member of the Tenoreno organized-crime family. He's taken over the business while his father awaits trial for the murder of his mother. Has he followed in Daddy's footsteps by attempting to kill his ex-wife?

Daniel Rosco—A member of the Rosco organized-crime family, lifelong partners with the Tenorenos. His parents were both recently murdered by the Tenorenos.

Fred Snell—An old bachelor who seems to know a lot about what's going on in his town. Does he have secrets of his own?

Prologue

Austin, Texas, five years ago

Sissy Jorgenson-Tenoreno attempted a smile at her friends to make the empty parking lot less spooky. It didn't work. "This is an odd place to meet, even for Xander."

The food truck's inside lights were glowing. So were the Christmas lights strung around the single picnic table out front. Daddy Cade's Po'Boys didn't seem to be one of the more popular gourmet trucks in town. Good thing she'd brought her entourage of Darren, Janna and Linda with her.

Xander should think twice if he thought she'd meet him anywhere alone.

"Your soon-to-be ex-husband probably chose this place because he knew you'd never eat here," Darren said. "You make every calorie count twice. Especially now that you need your figure back."

She was still the same size as when they'd

eloped eight months ago. In fact, the outfit she was wearing had been bought on their unofficial honeymoon trip to Paris.

"Sissy Jorgenson shouldn't be forced to come to a place like this," Janna complained. "You should send the police for your things. Even the cat."

Xander's father owns the police.

Did it really bother her that they talked as if they understood the life she'd led before getting married? Teen model, then married to the mob? They had no clue. Not really. A different location every week was glamorous to them. A different hotel each week was appealing. A life of travel and what appeared to be one party after another.

Even the parties got old. The same faces night after night. There weren't any sleepy movie days in front of the television. No study binges, no spontaneous orders of pizza and beer. No darting to the store for milk and bread, which were never on the menu anyway.

One day someone might ask what had been going through her mind when she got married. Her friends shrugged the divorce off as if it was no big deal. What had she expected? Happily ever after? Looking back, she hadn't really expected anything. She might not have known what marriage would be like, but she knew what she wanted.

The answer was so simple. She'd wanted a home. A place to belong, a family and a pet.

She'd never had one and always wanted to save the strays she saw while traveling. Instead, being married was equivalent to being locked inside a mansion surrounded by people who had no love in their hearts.

"I need a bottle of water or maybe this place sells Gel Shots. Five or six of those and we'll be ready to party again." Linda staggered across the gravel parking lot to the food truck and banged on the window. When no one answered, she swayed back to the group. "I'm so envious. In three days you'll be jet-setting halfway across the world for a fabulous Roman adventure. I, on the other hand, will be starting another boring semester of school."

While starving herself to drop down to her agent's ideal weight, she'd be wishing every minute for her friend's boring life.

"Anybody want a fried oyster po'boy? Of course Sissy's answer is no. She can't waste calories on stinky food. The bun alone would be—"

Sissy tuned them out and let them make fun of the way she'd eaten while staying with them over the past two months. They didn't understand that drastic measures were needed if she wanted her career back.

Even at the same weight there was the perception of what her body should be. She had to be thinner, taller, sleeker—more everything—to get back on top of the heap of girls who came along every day.

Fortunately, she hadn't been out of the paparazzi's eye very long. Her husband had made certain she'd been on his arm for special events. The press asked if she planned to return to her career after the honeymoon was over. Xander had assured them several times that their life would be a never-ending honeymoon.

But Xander Tenoreno was a liar and horrible person. If there was a villain in her life, it would be him. She was walking away from the divorce almost destitute. She'd been a dumb kid and rushed into marriage without a prenup. He'd taken everything. They'd been playing whose divorce attorney was the toughest until she'd realized that she could start over if she walked away.

It didn't matter. All she wanted was Miss Kitty, mainly to save her from the wrath of the household. None of the family was happy about the divorce. They didn't believe in it and took 'till death do you part' very literally.

No matter what Xander said or did, he couldn't keep her down. He could keep all of the money. According to her agent, she was still in high demand because of the public life she'd led, but she was almost *old* in model years. Old and only just celebrating her twenty-first birthday next week.

She looked around at the isolated parking lot and wondered if Xander was trying to frighten her. He didn't have to try hard. Would Xander or his family stoop to something that would hurt her friends? She shook her head, answering herself. Even they wouldn't be that public.

"What happened between you two, Sissy? Why did your Mr. Hunky-poo start sleeping around? He was so much fun to party with." Linda asked, hands on her hips, expecting an answer.

Okay, everyone in the parking lot expected an answer. After all, her life was continually up for discussion. Her every move was up for debate.

The threats and demands had been plentiful after their wedding vows but she hadn't told anyone. Not a soul. Not even her attorney. "I was supposed to stay at the mansion and be traipsed out whenever he needed someone to hang on his arm. It wasn't my scene."

"Barefoot, pregnant and cooking over a hot stove? You?" Janna laughed and everyone joined in.

That scenario would never have happened, but it was close. Of course she didn't get pregnant. Then a dozen doctors all agreed that there was no reason they couldn't have children. The consensus was that they shouldn't be in such a hurry. Give it time. But Xander had just quit. He tended to want immediate gratification for everything he did. People seemed to show up injured if he didn't.

"I don't have to think about that anymore." She

laced her fingers, then pulled them apart, sitting on them to keep still. *He can't hurt me if I'm not there.*

The Tenoreno family wanted her out of the way. Gone. Forever.

As long as he'd finally agreed to give her Miss Kitty, she could leave Texas and never look back. She looked around at the isolated food trailer. No other cars. No parking lot lights. It was just such an odd place for a man who liked everything shiny and new.

Including his women.

"It's eight forty-five. How long do we have to wait? That new band is opening at the Bat House. Is he always this late?" Darren paced.

"Yes. Time means nothing to him." She'd never thought he'd be here on the dot. But if roles were reversed and she was the one late, he would euthanize Miss Kitty as he'd threatened more than once to keep Sissy in line.

A super big SUV drove by. Smoke curled from the dark windows as it slowed. The bass of the music inside echoed through her chest it was so loud. Her friends danced to the hip-hop rhythm.

"We need music," Janna said, dancing to the fading beat over to the food truck window. "Come on. Can't you open up for a second? Even for water?"

Sissy swatted at her neck and shivered. It felt like something was crawling on her. Or maybe someone had walked on her grave. Wasn't that the saying? She discovered a tendril of her long hair had blown free from its intricate braid and tickled her skin. Her imagination had gone super wild.

As if she wasn't already scared enough. Now the thought of spiders in her hair had her all itchy. Another vehicle approached the three-way intersection with the same low bass thump. Another SUV?

Was it her imagination or an odd premonition that made her stand and move to the side of the trailer? She didn't know. But as the SUV drew even with the lot, she saw the gun barrel in the open window. She screamed. She dialed the number she'd had ready on her cell since they'd arrived.

The gunfire was maddeningly loud. She tried to get to the car. The gravel popped up in front of her hitting her legs first one direction and then the other. They shot all around her, missing. She was their target. She didn't doubt that for a second.

"Nine-one-one, what's your emergency?"

The voice was drowned out by more rapid fire of another weapon. Laughter from the men as they opened the car doors. She wanted to recognize one of the men who followed the Tenoreno family everywhere. She couldn't be certain. But the family wanted her out of the way.

Gone. Forever.

There was nowhere to run. No one to call out

to for help. She was about to die and wanted to scream louder. Scream hysterically.

The phone was still in her palm. She couldn't be certain the police would respond. Her husband might have paid them to avoid the area. She prayed someone decent was on the other end of the call, trying to discover what was happening in this remote parking lot.

The gunfire stopped.

Sissy looked up, blinking hard to see her attackers. Maybe they were just trying to scare—another burst. Linda's screams were cut off. Janna's followed. Her eyes never shut as she fell to the ground.

The stinging fire in her side whipped her around. Another stabbed through her arm like a hot knife through butter…quick, silently tearing her flesh. A third and fourth pierced under her arm that had flown above her head.

Darren wrapped his arms around her but they fell. She landed hard under him. His body protected her from the full force of the bullets. The white gravel that had been hard to walk through minutes earlier turned dark. It registered but there was no pain. She couldn't catch her breath, couldn't speak.

The phone wasn't in her hand. It had bounced away. The case had popped open, but the light was still on. Someone still listened.

It was interesting what registered in her mind

during those few life-ending seconds. Trivial information like the spots of blood now on the metal legs of the table. Or the burned-out bulb on the twinkle lights at the rear of the lot.

The noise of the bass hip-hop and guns faded away to be replaced by sirens.

What did any detail around her matter? She'd been shot…more than once. She was about to die. There was no one left to truly grieve for her. She'd said goodbye to a greedy family long ago. Her only friends were dead because she hadn't wanted to be alone to face her ex-husband.

After all their sacrifice, she would still die alone.

What good had she accomplished in her life? She knew how to walk in high heels and how to throw her hair over her shoulder before placing her hand on her hip.

Somehow she dragged her hand to her side and cried out from the pain. She wanted to tell someone the truth. Leave some sort of message about who had killed her. There wasn't a way to reach her phone. She couldn't move Darren.

Her last thought should have been about kittens or something good. Instead the only thing that repeated over and over again was a never-to-be-seen headline…

Xander Tenoreno Had Killed His Wife, Sissy Jorgenson, and No One Would Ever Know.

Chapter One

Hico, Texas, present day

"Shirtless? Of course I'm shirtless." Bryce Johnson yanked the muscle shirt over his head, catching it on his ear. "What legitimate undercover Texas Ranger mows a lawn trying to get a woman's attention wearing a shirt?"

"I bet you have your glasses on, too." There was a familiar sound from his partner, Jesse Ryder, as he held the phone to his chest and laughed. "And…um…don't forget your Sig is showing."

Bryce scrambled behind his back. He gave up and went inside to drop his weapon, shirt and glasses. He didn't need to see up close to mow the lawn anyway. The briskness of the AC helped cool his frustration. A little.

"You know…" Jesse continued laughing. "If just taking your shirt off doesn't work, you could try a speedo and a giant sombrero."

"Har har har."

Jesse should be giving him legitimate advice for his first undercover assignment. Not poking him with a big stick through the phone. It didn't matter. His partner was three for three this morning and it seemed like Bryce was about to strike out.

This weekend was his final at bat.

"Seriously, man, is there a problem? If you don't get her attention today, you might as well hang it up. They're going to pull the plug and move on."

"We don't know for a fact this is Tenoreno's ex-wife."

"Now, look, Bryce. You sold Major Parker on this assignment because you were certain this woman was the ex. What's changed your mind?"

"Nothing. But there's been no evidence or action that solidifies my hunch either."

"Hunch? Hunch?" Jesse's voice rose in decibels and octaves. "You know how important this is to me, pal. The state's attorney needs a slam dunk in the courtroom this fall. If this isn't the ex, you need to move on and find her. We don't have time for you to play a hunch."

The picture he'd burned into his memory could be a match. *Was* a match as far as he was concerned. He was certain. But short of walking up to her and asking if she had a bullet-wound scar on her abdomen and two others under her arm, there was no proof.

He needed proof or her admission since he

didn't want to ask her outright. He couldn't ask the time of day or to borrow a cup of sugar. Her house was secure and locked up tighter than the local bank.

"When I'm not fixing something on this rental—which was a part of the deal you hatched up—I'm spending my spare time running more searches. You can't guilt-trip me into working harder. I haven't had a day off in weeks."

"I know, man. We just don't have time to waste."

There was a lot more to this case than just finding a potential witness. The Tenoreno family had already tried to kill law officers to make the case fall apart. As far as they knew, the crime family was still searching for the primary witness under Company F protection.

"Then let me get back outside and come up with a way to introduce myself." He disconnected before his partner could try to give him more advice. His head was swimming with all the suggestions from the Rangers in his company.

He left his service weapon in the lockbox he'd brought with him last week. Short trips back to Waco down Texas 6 had yielded more than a couple of suitcases of his stuff. The house was furnished, but he'd brought items to make it livable. Including his television and game station.

Livable? More like bachelorized.

The July heat pounded on his shoulders as he

finished the outside chores. Not a bright idea for skin that hadn't seen the light of day in years. He'd listened to advice from another Texas Ranger about how to get a woman's attention, and today he was desperate.

Bryce was finally on an assignment that didn't include a computer. For the most part anyway. He was undercover. On his own and getting sunburned.

It had been a while since his back had seen the sun and done yardwork. Too long apparently. He'd just finished the lawn—the burning-dried-up-grass-with-no-trees-in-the-yard lawn. Patches of it were more dirt than the combo of overgrown weeds that he'd just plowed through.

If he didn't get closer to his target this weekend, his undercover time was done. Nothing he did and nowhere he'd been seemed to catch Kylie Scott's eye. Twice he'd been thrown next to her by town matchmakers. Twice they'd had polite conversation. Twice he'd been certain he'd broken through her protective shell. And twice he'd been wrong.

Holding his straw hat away from him, he turned the water hose on himself with the other. Spitting-hot water hit his skin but quickly soothed the burn. Probably wasn't good against sun protection, but he was just dang hot and wanted to cool down fast.

He also needed a minute to watch the house across the street and two doors down. She had been taking care of lawn maintenance on a Sat-

urday morning, too. Conservatively dressed in shorts and a long-sleeved shirt, Kylie Scott wasn't flashy. No bikini tops to work on her tan.

Pecan Street was empty now and Kylie's garage door was shut. He should put the yard tools away and return to the half-assed air-conditioning. He'd missed when she'd finished up and moved inside.

"Some undercover cop you turned out to be." He'd talked more to himself in the past week than he'd ever admit. The red shoulders were just going to get worse. He might as well head to the store and grab some ointment. Or maybe he could ask to borrow some from Kylie.

Taking a drink from the hose, he contemplated that until there was a puddle of mud next to him. How could he meet her?

Former teen supermodel Sissy Jorgenson, the ex-wife of a short-lived marriage to Xander Tenoreno was hiding and doing a damn good job of it. Her ex was the state's real target. It would help their case if they had more evidence against the Texas crime family and Company F had been assigned to obtain it.

Bottom line, Xander was also looking for his ex-bride. The rumor circulating was that she had evidence against him that had kept her alive. True or false, Bryce didn't know. His goal was to find Sissy/Kylie and convince her to hand over her evidence against the Tenorenos.

Head of the family, Paul Tenoreno, was behind

bars without bail facing trial in September. The final blow would be to add his son Xander as a cellmate. Bryce soaked his head, then shook his hair from side to side. Water sprayed like his brother's dog shaking after swimming in their pool.

"As good as that feels, you might not want to greet your neighbors that way."

He recognized Kylie's voice, spun around. She screamed a little and hopped backward. He'd soaked her shirt with the water hose.

"Dammit, that was careless of me. Sorry." Bryce wiped his eyes free of droplets still clinging to his skin.

"Wow, that was a bit of a shock." She fanned her shirt front, but didn't run home.

"I, uh…didn't hear you come up."

"I hope so, because if you wanted to have a wet T-shirt contest… Well, you'd need a shirt." She nodded toward him, wringing the edge of her shirt onto her multicolored toenails.

Wait. What? Was she flirting with him?

Without his glasses and with water dripping into his eyes, he could barely see her facial expression, just her bright smile. True wheat-blond hair was pulled into a ponytail and stuck through the back of a ball cap. She was the right height of about five feet eleven. She wasn't rail-thin, but slender enough to be a teenage model who had left the business.

"Come to think about it, we probably do have

some guys on this street who wouldn't mind serving as the judges. You'd win of course."

"Huh? Oh. Right." He couldn't think of anything to say.

"You're making a bigger puddle." She pointed to his feet.

Bryce jumped toward the faucet and turned off the water, cursing under his breath at his ineptness. He slowly stood, ready to see where this strange encounter would lead.

"Bryce? I don't mean to impose, but I need your help. That is, if you could spare a few minutes."

"I don't have any plans."

She relaxed and let out a long sigh. "Oh good. It shouldn't take long. I noticed that you have an extension ladder and wondered if you could get my pole saw out of the tree in my backyard."

"Sure." *Flirting?* Wishful thinking was more like it.

He retrieved the ladder from the garage and headed down the middle of the small town street.

"Need help?"

"Not at all, I got this."

She was already walking next to him as if she'd known how he would answer. The ladder was more awkward than heavy. Sort of like their conversation. He had an opportunity now and couldn't think of anything he might ask that wouldn't sound suspicious.

Last thing he needed was for her to take off

and disappear. He'd never hear the end of that at the office.

"I've noticed that you don't talk much."

"Not really. If I'm honest, I haven't gotten much practice lately." He rested the ladder on the inside of her fence as she worked the combination lock on the gate. If she wasn't the former Sissy Tenoreno, something had happened to Kylie Scott to make her overcautious.

"Are we being honest?" She smiled shyly, focusing on removing the lock.

The temperature should have dropped when they walked under the oak shade tree. But he could swear it rose several degrees when she stole a look before she pushed up her sunglasses.

In the past couple of weeks, he'd never seen her eyes up close. Even without his glasses, her long eyelashes, tinted a rich dark brown, hadn't hidden the quick peek she'd taken of his chest.

Instead of the bright blue eyes from her modeling days, they were a deep dark brown—almost black—when she didn't hide behind mirrored shades. Definitely not the color of Sissy's, but the shape...

No doubt remained.

Kylie Scott was the woman he'd been searching for.

KYLIE OPENED THE gate and Bryce grabbed the ladder on the other side. She dropped the lock back

through the slots, then removed it before he noticed—hopefully. It was silly to be so paranoid.

But paranoia had taught her to be hypervigi-
lant with her safety. She wasn't used to leaving
the locks out of place.

Even when no one appeared to be on the street.
Even when she had a very capable-looking man
standing next to her, it went against her habits to
leave the gate unlocked. But she managed it by
sticking the padlock inside her pocket.

"I was trimming a dead limb and the saw got
stuck."

"Lucky I was around."

"I have some iced tea. Can I get you some?"

"That would be great."

"Okay." She rubbed her palms together and
stepped to the porch. She tried to turn her back
on Bryce and walk like a normal person through
her kitchen door.

It didn't happen. She hesitated, waiting for him
to lean the ladder on the tree. He just watched her
act like an unsteady idiot. Bryce was practically
a stranger. She'd only met him a couple of times
in town.

"I hope you like it sweetened. That's all I have."

"Sure. I'll get this down."

"Thanks so much. It's stuck up there pretty
good." Oh my gosh. She was babbling, trying to
wait him out. If he'd just look away, she could dart
into the kitchen.

Kylie had never been a normal teenage girl, but she was certain this was how they acted. Flushed, embarrassed, unsure of themselves— everything that she was experiencing for the first time. She'd been a full-time employee by the time she'd reached puberty. The boys she'd known back then had never been mature enough for her tastes.

Needless to say, the men who accepted her as an adult at that age hadn't been good for her. Well, spilled milk and all that...whatever the saying was. She'd moved past it. She was in a good place and didn't have to think about that any longer.

Throwing her shoulders back, she turned, leaving herself vulnerable to a nonexistent attack. She slid the glass door open and marched to the refrigerator for the pitcher. Two glasses sat on a pretty little tray she'd picked up at the antique shop this week. She added a freshly sliced lemon to a matching bowl and poured the tea.

Five years. She'd survived five years. Her life was changing and it was time to keep her promise to herself. If she could survive this long without being discovered, it was time to start living again.

Taking a second, she watched Bryce tug on the pole trying to free the tiny saw. He arranged the ladder soundly in place, shook it a little to see if it was steady, then climbed.

It had been a very long time since she'd allowed herself friends. Then again, being Bryce's friend wasn't too high on her agenda. She'd watched him

out in the yard fixing up Mrs. Mackey's rental. He'd stopped by the pie shop while she'd been at lunch.

It might be a coincidence, but Hico was a very small town. If there was a visitor here for a couple of hours, a resident was likely to encounter them a couple of times. So running into a neighbor at the store and pie shop was almost predictable.

She hadn't been the only woman catching a second or third glimpse of his straight nose and dimpled chin. A constant five o'clock shadow had never done anything for her before getting a look at Bryce. She was full-blown giddily attracted to every muscle his tight T-shirts exploited.

The view as he climbed the ladder wasn't helping to cool her heat.

Mrs. Mackey had praised Bryce's ability as a handyman and suggested his skills not be wasted while he was living on their street. At face value her statement had been so innocent. Then the other ladies who had conveniently stopped by the museum had all giggled.

"If they could see you right now, they'd probably faint or have heart attacks. They definitely would if they knew what my plans for him are." She took the dish towel and fanned her flaming cheeks. Dipping her head, she closed her eyes, embarrassed by her desires. "What are you thinking, Kylie? Yes, it's been a while. But you can't just ask him to bed. You deserve more than that."

With her mind made up to slow her racing thoughts, she met her helpful neighbor at the bottom of the ladder. He stepped onto the grass, tree trimmer in hand, following her to two chairs and a small patio table—her fourth anniversary present to herself.

No matter what she kept telling her mind to do, she couldn't avoid the manly chest turning a feminine shade of pink. He took a sip of tea, then gulped it down.

"That's really good. Just hit the spot."

"Thanks again for the help, Bryce. If you hadn't been home, I'd be watching that pole saw rust."

"I doubt that, but anytime." He tipped his straw hat in her direction.

"That's interesting."

"What?"

"The hat-tipping thing. No one under the age of sixty has ever tipped their hat to me before. In fact, I'd never seen it until I moved to Hico. People wave when they pass in their cars. They acknowledge me on the sidewalk. They even open the museum door, wave and go on their way."

"I'd say they're just being friendly." He finished off his tea and set the glass down.

"It's the reason I stayed here. I hadn't planned on it, but I'm glad I did."

"That's right. You work in the Billy the Kid Museum." He took another long gulp of his tea.

"I used to make my brother pretend he was Billy the Kid when we were practicing quick draw."

That's what she wanted...to be so relaxed and easy going. She sipped. It had been five years. Maybe it was possible? "And who would you pretend to be?"

"The sheriff."

"Why not the outlaw? I thought kids wanted to be the cool gunslinger who shot things up?" She noticed he actually looked a little embarrassed. "Did you play cops and robbers, too?"

"I think I got in trouble one too many times for shooting birds with my BB gun. Too many lectures on how I should be a better example. Besides, the good guys always win."

"I've heard that."

Before she could think again if she was the good or the bad, she heard his cell vibrate.

He jumped to his feet and reached into his back pocket. "Excuse me a second, I have to take this."

Kylie tried not to listen. Maybe it was a habit mixed with genuine curiosity, but she felt uncomfortable and moved out of earshot to the tree. It wasn't difficult to discern the phone call was upsetting to Bryce. His side of the conversation was a lot of one-word responses. His body language became very stiff and formal. She sipped her tea, looking at the dead limb that still needed to be trimmed back to the trunk.

When he returned, Bryce dropped his hands to his knees, bending at the waist to lean forward.

Kylie set her glass down, approaching cautiously. No matter how much she wanted to know this man, she didn't. That was a fact that she couldn't push aside. "Is something wrong?"

"Everything, I'm afraid. Someone couldn't do their job correctly and my timetable's been advanced." He straightened.

The sadness and concern didn't belong on his handsome features. The urge to wipe them aside was too strong to ignore. She recognized it and held it in a secret place where she kept most of her emotions.

"I'm sorry, Bryce. I hope things work out for the best."

"I hope so, too. There's something you should know, Kylie." Bryce rested his hands on his hips. "If I can find you…so can Xander Tenoreno."

Chapter Two

Kylie could feel the blood drain from her face as fast as it had in her knees. Barely able to stand, she sort of rocked before catching herself on the tree trunk. Her ex-husband's name hadn't been said in front of her for almost four years. She wanted to run. Hide.

Bryce watched her reaction. He saw it all. She knew what the fright looked like and she hadn't hidden it. The look on his face confirmed for her that he knew he'd found the right person. She couldn't deny it. Well, she could, but it wouldn't do her any good. He wouldn't believe her.

"Are you a cop?"

He shook his head, squinted, then rubbed the back of his neck as if he was mad for being right. An odd reaction from someone who had completely wrecked her life.

She looked at the serving tray and the ceramic outdoor table it sat on. Neither would cross over to

her new life. Whatever that ended up being. Just the things that fit inside two suitcases. Nothing more. Not even the laptop. She couldn't borrow a car. He'd just follow.

Everything stayed here.

The escape plan was in place. The cash was in a box under the bathroom sink along with a passible ID. All she had to do was fake whatever Mr. Unbelievable standing in front of her wanted.

"If you worked for Xander, I'd already be dead. So who are you?" All the excitement of finally having the courage to face Bryce sort of evaporated along with any moisture in the heated air.

"Bryce Johnson. I'm a Texas Ranger here to help you."

"Help me right out of my comfortable home and life you mean." She picked up the tea glasses, along with the tray. Another wave of sadness crashed into her heart at the thought of leaving. "It was that silly picture for the online article, wasn't it?"

He nodded. "And your eyes. You changed the color but not the vitality that's there."

"Strange words from a man who probably just got me killed." She walked across the porch, the lock heavy in her pocket. The urge to run to the fence and secure the gate made her stop before opening the door. Bryce was following and paused on the steps.

"We can help you, if you allow us to."

"I told the police, and anyone else who would listen, everything that happened that night." The nightmare images forced her to stare at a pure drop of water sliding down the empty glass. If she shut her eyes or even blinked, she'd be transported back to the white gravel stained with blood.

"Kylie."

Startled by the shock of his touch, she dropped the tray. One glass shattered and one rolled across the wooden porch. "Isn't that weird? Ever wonder why sometimes they break and sometimes they don't?"

"All the time." He knelt beside her to pick up the broken pieces. "I didn't mean to scare you."

"What did you expect when you announced that my ex could find me? Is he really looking again?"

Their eyes met and held as he asked, "Again?"

Nice eyes. Such a shame.

Kylie mentally shook it off. None of the attraction was real. He was a flippin' Texas Ranger and not the good-looking handyman across the street. He was here with sneaky ulterior motives. She stood, confused by all the emotions making her want to cry.

Not in front of him, though. She would not cry until she was on a bus heading to the airport. No one cared if she cried on the bus.

She carefully balanced the tray on the wooden porch rail and took a step toward the door. "Who was on the call you took and what did they say?"

"Austin PD."

Her fingers wrapped around the screen door's handle. "My case never made it to court. They assured me there was a lack of evidence. I have no idea what you're referring to or why you're here. So why don't you just cut to the part where you've put my life in danger."

"Are you aware your father-in-law—"

"Ex-father-in-law."

"Right. Look, Miss Jorgenson."

"Wrong again. My name is Kylie Scott. Sissy Jorgenson died with the first bullet. She doesn't exist anymore." She took advantage of Bryce's awkward silence. He politely backed up to allow her to get inside and wedge the screen between them.

A good hostess would open the screen farther and invite him into the kitchen. The hot July air was thick and getting hotter. A bead of sweat rolled across her skin and wedged between her breasts, squeezed together by her sports bra.

Her voice and body might appear to be calm, but she was hyperaware of every second of panic she stopped from bubbling to the surface. Knees about to buckle, she wanted to run inside and leave the handsome Texas Ranger locked out on her stoop.

Bryce took off his hat, getting closer to the screen. He raised his hand toward the handle, but changed his mind at the last minute.

"I'm not sure what I can say. It was never my intention to use scare tactics to get you to listen to me. I wanted you to trust me before I had to tell you."

"That was never going to happen. I can't—won't—trust anyone like that again. You're wasting your time. Not to mention the taxpayers' dollars." She let the screen shut but didn't make a move to close the inner door. Why was she was putting off the inevitable?

Maybe she didn't want to leave. Or shoot, it really was because his concerned look crinkled the corner of his eyes. And he looked different without his glasses. Maybe that wasn't concern and he just couldn't focus.

Whatever the reason, he'd taken his hat off and his hair had a cute little flip where his hat had rested. He was seriously adorable-looking—whether guys liked to be thought of that way or not. And yes, she didn't want to shut the door in his face.

"The gentlemanly thing for you to do is leave now." She edged the door closed a little more.

"You're right. Leaving would be polite. But right now, I'm a Texas Ranger…not a gentleman."

The screen popped open and her reflexes moved her backward into the kitchen. He was through the door quickly, shutting it and turning the dead bolt. Once that was done he turned to her, hat in hand, bare-chested and terribly sunburned.

"You'll forgive me, Kylie. I've got my orders and I need to make sure you're clear on a few facts." He gestured to the small table in the corner. She joined him. "You see, someone—we assume Tenoreno—is actively looking for you. His father is in jail awaiting trial for murdering his mother."

"I heard. Don't you think I keep up with them?"

"What you might not know is that we think Xander doesn't want his father cleared. He's taking over the family business. He also knows that we're building a case against him. You can help strengthen the state's case." He leaned forward on his knees, slowly spinning that silly straw hat brim through his fingers.

"No. No. No. A thousand times no. I don't have any evidence to help you. Don't you think I tried that before the divorce? If I could have blackmailed him for my freedom, I would have."

"The rumors aren't true, then." He totally looked the part of a workingman. Somebody who fixed things for a living. He's not, she reminded herself, staying angry. He deceived her and all the residents of Hico.

"Does Mrs. Mackey know you're a cop?" She placed both her feet flat on the ground and sat straight in her chair. She knew all about body language and she was being as inhospitable as possible.

"Not a cop."

"Is there a difference?"

"Technicalities mostly. Honor. A code that's hard to understand." He set the hat on one knee and leaned back against the vinyl chair.

She understood all too well why he winced. It was the reason she wore a special UV-protected shirt with long sleeves. "I have some aloe that will help that burn."

"I'll be okay. If you wouldn't mind answering a few questions about the Tenorenos—" He pulled free of the chair, gritting his teeth so hard the muscles jumped in his jaw.

"I'll be right back."

Summing up her options had become second nature. She hadn't been spontaneous in five lonely years. It had taken over an hour to decide to ask Bryce to retrieve her pole saw.

Should she grab the handgun she'd hidden in the bathroom in case of a bad situation like this?

It should have already been decided. She'd weighed all the variables when she'd bought the gun and learned how to use it. If Bryce hadn't been in the house, she'd be talking to herself, debating. But he was in the house and he'd most likely leave if she just asked.

That was the rub. She hadn't asked.

Why? She was ready to move past living this way and had made the decision after she'd met him last week. That's why. He was already part of an idea that would rescue her from her routine.

She looked at herself in the bathroom mirror. The gun was in a hidden compartment behind a picture. It had taken her weeks to build it herself. The result was amateurish, but it was covered by a frame and no one knew about it.

Pulling the aloe from the cupboard, she longed to be brave or a little fearless. It had been quite a while since she'd felt like life was to be lived with reckless abandon.

"Get lost?" Bryce's deep voice penetrated her body like a shock. He stood at the edge of the kitchen. He hadn't followed.

Her breath caught in her throat like an air bubble or hiccup. Maybe it was more like trying not to cry. Whatever it was, she was uncertain and confused. There was no reason to automatically trust this man.

No reason to help him with answers about the Tenorenos or his sunburn.

Bottle of lotion in hand, she turned to his smiling pink face confident that she'd thought out her plan a thousand times and it was the right thing to do. She shoved the lotion into his chest. He caught it with one hand while the other held on to his hat.

"As much as I want to celebrate five years of freedom, I know that I'll never be free from the Tenoreno family. I had hopes but nothing will change that. So I'd like you to leave, Bryce. Just go away."

BRYCE HAD BEEN asked to leave. As a Texas Ranger, he should. As a man who had delivered news that clearly upset this woman…he couldn't.

"You have no reason to trust me, Kylie." He watched her chest rise, inhaling air to state her defense and pushed on before she could. "I do see why trusting anyone would be almost impossible. You asked me what the difference was between a cop and a Texas Ranger. We don't have an agenda."

"I'd still like you to leave and I think you have to now."

"I'm not leaving until I explain."

"I wish you wouldn't." She flattened against the wall.

Was she afraid? She should be. Her ex-husband was turning out to be as bad and deceptive as his father. "Xander Tenoreno lost the police detail this morning. There's a chance he could be headed here."

He wondered how Kylie had ever managed to fool anyone about her fake history. With every mention of her ex's name she paled and practically became a different person. Her entire demeanor changed. Now was no different, her eyes darted to the bath, her hand rubbed her side—probably one of the bullet-wound scars.

"You told Xander so you could get me to do your bidding. You're all the same. Out only for your own selfish interests—"

"Kylie!" He raised his voice and reached for her wrist.

A couple of seconds later, the bottle of lotion she'd given him went flying against the wall and he was lying on his back wondering how he'd been outmaneuvered.

"Oh my God, I'm so sorry. I've done that in practice, but never...I didn't mean to—oh, no." Kylie knelt next to him alternating between a pat on his shoulder and his head.

"You've been taking...martial arts." He needed a second to get his lungs working correctly.

"Aikido. It just sort of kicked in. I knew I was nervous. I guess I should have tried to calm down." She covered her mouth. "Can you get up?"

"I think I'll just wait here for a second."

She smiled. It was worth being knocked to his back to see her relax enough to smile like that.

"You know, I never thought it would work. The moves are so practiced and mechanical. This is really sort of cool."

"Tell that to my back."

"I'm so sorry. Are you going to be okay?" Her touch was cooling to his burning skin.

"All but my pride. If that's an auto response, I'd hate to see what you can do when you're deliberately provoked."

"I'd probably freeze in my tracks." She looked comfortable. His knees would be screaming sitting bent like that.

"Is that why you have a gun stashed back there?"

"What? How did you know?"

"Your reaction." He rose to one elbow. "The way you keep looking in that direction. You almost twitched."

Her blond hair framed her face as she leaned forward. "I can see that I need to practice my self-control."

"Well you sure as hell don't need to practice throwing a man to the ground. That was more than a little embarrassing."

"Part of aikido is to react without thinking. Defending yourself without giving away what you're about to do. I've practiced during class, but there hasn't been any reason to actually use it here in Hico."

"Until now." He stretched his back, confident everything was still in one piece. "I didn't mean to make you feel threatened."

"The only thing you did was reemphasize my reality. I was fooling myself thinking things would change."

She was retreating again. Talking behind her hand, wrapping the other around her waist. He wasn't going to let her demonstrate more aikido to make her feel better. He pulled himself to a sitting position and leaned against the wall.

"Can you hand me that lotion? Maybe rub some on my back and shoulders before I go?"

"Okay, guy from down the street, you're def-

initely ready to leave." She tossed the bottle to his gut.

He trapped it, squeezed some of the green goo on his palm and slapped his shoulder. "I really could use some help."

"You managed to get burned all by yourself."

"You're joking, but the reason I'm burned is because I was trying to impress you."

She scooted on her knees to be next to him, extending her hand. He swiped the lotion onto her fingers. She squirted a lot more across his shoulders, the sudden chill made him wince.

What a change a couple of minutes made. She'd been so frightened that she'd flipped him to his back with a defensive move and now she was rubbing aloe on his shoulders. She'd also gone from petrified to smiling.

"My research might have given an indication of who we were searching for, triggering someone else's search. I trust everyone who I'm directly involved with in this case. But some parts of it are out of my control. I didn't mean to lead your ex-husband to you."

The light rubbing across his shoulders slowed for a second. Kylie spread the aloe, remaining silent behind him with her face and expressions hidden. He didn't want her to be nervous again. He preferred her smiling. So did his back.

"Your aikido. That was a great move. What's it called?"

"Aiki otoshi. It's a blending drop. I like it because you don't have to lift or flip your opponent."

"I noticed that. You hit my knees together and there wasn't anything I could do to stop the fall. You're good. That wasn't a beginner's move."

She moved away, replacing the cap to the lotion. "Keep it."

"Even though I didn't mean to put you in danger, I think you need to come with me, Kylie. We can keep you safe."

They were sitting on the floor. She'd created a corner where she could see both doors, but was protected from anyone looking inside by the couch and walls. He noticed the mirrors strategically hung on the wall and one on a bookshelf.

Kylie Scott had a lot of precautions in place. She'd studied self-defense and probably was a crack shot with whatever weapon she had hidden in her bathroom. But it still wasn't a match for a man with endless resources and contacts like her ex-husband.

"You didn't see anything while you lived in the house? Is there any place he might keep important files?" he asked.

"I don't mean to be insensitive, but didn't the murders earlier this year get you inside that bleak mansion?"

"Only relating to the murders. The Tenorenos' lawyers made certain of that."

"Look, Bryce. I know you think you can protect

me. You may really want to. But we both know it's just not true. At some point you'll have to walk away and I'll be alone. I can't worry about other people. I have to think about staying alive."

"Come to Waco. Let the attorneys run some questions past you. We'll keep it confidential. No one will know, but you might be able to help us shut down their operation."

"Stop it. I wasn't around their daily deals with lowlifes. When I stayed there I was kept from everything. No one helped me. Isabella was such a nice woman, but never on my side. It was her son one hundred percent." Kylie stood and pointed toward the door.

"You don't have to face this alone." He got to his feet, making one last plea. "We can help you put him away for the murders of your friends."

She covered her face with both hands. She looked up with determination, shaking her head.

"You said Xander wanted to take over the business. He doesn't need to find me to do that. He never believed in divorce and couldn't stand the idea that I would leave him. Plain and simple, as soon as I left him, he wanted me dead."

Chapter Three

"I know she's going to run. What do you want me to do about it?" Bryce had taken only enough time to change his clothes. The aloe on his shoulders helped the initial sting, but he should have worn a T-shirt. Now was not the time to be concerned about sunburn pain.

"Follow her," Major Parker said firmly. "You're certain she understands the consequences of rejecting our offer of protection?"

"Yes, sir." He rubbed his lower back. "She thinks she can take care of herself."

"It was good work finding her, Johnson. Real good work."

"Thank you, sir."

I just hope she doesn't get killed.

Hico, Texas wasn't large. It wasn't even a medium-sized town. If Kylie Scott was headed out of town, she really was at a crossroads to head

in any direction. She'd given him no indication where that might be.

Maybe he could rule out east to Waco. Northeast toward Fort Worth and an international airport? Northwest to Stephenville and too many small towns to name? Or southwest to Mexico? There wasn't a warrant. No reason to detain her. No legal reason to keep her from running.

Whichever direction she decided, it would be today. He'd seen that look in her eyes. Panicked with a plan. She was leaving, all right. And it looked like her ride had just pulled up.

The old Chevy pickup stopped by Kylie's house most afternoons. She worked two part-time jobs and the older man gave her rides. Bryce had met her at the Billy the Kid Museum downtown where she walked a mile to work three days a week.

The other job he'd heard about from Mrs. Mackey. Fred Snell drove her to ranches right outside town where she worked cleaning barns with teens who needed community service. Mrs. Mackey had elaborated that Kylie was a good listener.

This afternoon she looked like every afternoon she hitched a ride. Nothing more than a small backpack in her hand and a pair of work gloves. But he'd seen that look.

Fred backed up out of the driveway. Without a plan of what he was going to do, Bryce stepped off his porch and jogged to the street. He waved

Fred over. Kylie glared at him, but rolled down the window.

"Hey, Kylie. Mr. Snell, I think Mrs. Mackey introduced us at the café last Wednesday. Nice to see you again." The older gent bobbed his head. "I was wondering if you could use another hand."

"What's that? I'm a little hard of hearing."

"He asked if he could come with us today." Kylie shook her head.

Fred looked around her and squinted at the window. "Yeah, you're Mackey's handyman. We can always use another pair of young hands and a strong back. We're clearing some brush out at the Childerses's. Scoot over to the middle, Kylie."

"I don't think this is a good idea, Fred." She looked from one man to the other. Bryce could tell she was scrambling for an excuse to not open the door. "He needs gloves and has a horrible sunburn. He might get sick from it."

"Nonsense, Kylie. I have lots of extra gloves. You hand 'em out to the kids. Plenty of men work when their shoulders are red. Besides, you make us use sunscreen." He nodded and the debate was over.

Kylie scooted while he opened the door. Her eyes shot daggers—no other way to describe it—into Bryce's heart. He should be a dead man after those sharp points had stabbed him multiple times.

Fred stepped on the gas and the old truck

chugged as loud as a train down Pecan Street. "Might as well leave that window down, son. AC went out in this thing back in '79."

There wasn't much small talk between the roar of the engine and the wind blowing through the cab. He dropped his arm behind Kylie to make a little more room and ended up with an elbow in his ribs.

"Ouch. What was that for?"

"The least you could have done is left your gun at home. I'm surprised you're not wearing a white hat since you're trying to come to my rescue." She wiggled on the old vinyl seat, trying to gain space between their hips.

"Now, Kylie, darlin', I'm going to downshift in a few. Scoot back over to our new volunteer." Fred kept his eyes straight ahead, one elbow out the window and one hand on the wheel.

One look at his upturned lips and anyone could tell he thought he was helping two lovebirds take flight. Fred hadn't been exaggerating about shifting soon. They turned taking a road that was more dust than dirt.

Their driver rolled up his window and Bryce took the hint. It was better to sweat and be able to breathe.

"Want to take off your extra shirt?" he asked close to Kylie's ear.

She shook her head and pulled the long-sleeve shirt closed at the neck. In the past two weeks he

hadn't seen her in short sleeves. *Battle scars*. She'd been shot four times in that drive-by.

They reached their destination and Bryce would have a hard time if he had to drive back by himself. His shirt was sticking to his skin. He winced when Kylie lightly patted him between his shoulders.

"Thanks for coming to help," she said loudly.

Fred acknowledged and gave a wave to follow. Other cars and trucks were close by. A few young people milled around the corner of the house, coming to attention when Fred approached.

"I thought you worked with a couple of kids cleaning barns."

"Today is special. A tornado came through the property in the spring and we need to clear it out. The Childers family has donated the wood to the teen group. They plan to sell it for firewood."

"Know how to use a chain saw, son?" Fred asked from where three were being gassed up.

"Yes, sir. Grew up around them."

"Grab a pair of gloves from behind the seat and come get a refresher. We don't allow anyone who hasn't graduated to use one." He pointedly turned to the kid at his elbow and shook his head.

"You don't have to do this, you know." Kylie threw her bag over her shoulder and pulled her gloves on.

She acted like running away was the furthest thing from her mind. No one would have guessed

that she wasn't moving through her life like normal. Her biggest worry at the moment seemed to be how they'd get all the wood back to town.

Xander Tenoreno was out there. No one was watching him. He could be meeting with a hired gun, sending one of his men or planning—yeah, he could be planning to take care of his ex-wife himself. Bryce had seen some of the gruesome results the Texas Mafia families had left in their wake. How could he convince her to come with him?

"Kylie, why don't you take Bryce, Calvert and Martin on your team. Everybody clear on the rules?" Fred asked.

"What rules?" He nudged Kylie before she could walk too far away.

"The team that stacks the most wood wins a bunch of donations from the town. Daydreaming isn't allowed...we want to win. Right, guys?"

"Whatever," they both answered, clearly not excited.

"Martin, do you mind lugging this thing and taking Bryce to the worksite? I need to say hi to Mrs. Childers."

"No prob."

Bryce was torn. He needed to keep Kylie in sight. Whatever her plan, she wasn't leaving without her shoulder bag. "Why don't I carry this for you?"

"That's all right. No need."

"I insist." He took it off her arm, playing a little tug-of-war until she let go.

"Fine." She ran up the hill to the house joining a woman on the porch.

As much as he wanted to hear that conversation, he felt it was necessary to maintain his cover story with Kylie's friends. If she announced he was a Texas Ranger...who would show up on her doorstep?

Then again, what if that was what the conversation was right at this moment?

"YOU'RE CERTAIN IT will be okay?" Kylie asked.

"Of course I am. I'll explain everything to Richard later. He'll take the grandkids in the four wheeler and catch Little Bit tomorrow. No big deal. They'll have a blast."

"I can't tell you how much I appreciate this, Lisa."

"On the other hand, maybe you should tell me what's wrong. You aren't afraid of the tall and good-looking one over there. Are you? Is that what this is all about?"

"No. I don't want to involve him." She watched the last of the teams disappear into the trees.

"Well, maybe you should. He looks like someone who could fix a couple of problems."

"Remember, we just talked about ordering pizza for the kids and getting water down the hill."

"I'll have Little Bit saddled and ready to go at

four, but I don't understand why you're all set to visit the Turners. I could run you over in the car a lot faster."

"I've been looking forward to my ride on Little Bit all week and I don't want Fred to miss out on his pizza. So I'll hop the fence and walk. I love to walk. Jan said she didn't mind bringing me home."

Kylie took a couple of steps away and realized this might be the last time she'd see Lisa. She ran back to the bottom step and threw her arms around the older woman's neck. She never hugged, but the people in Hico had helped her in so many ways.

"I'm a better person for knowing you and all my friends here. You guys have been so good to me. Thanks."

Lisa didn't let go. "You've got me a little scared now, Kylie. What have you gotten yourself into?"

She'd practiced this laugh in the mirror a thousand times when she'd been modeling. Her carefree, nothing-in-the-world-matters laugh that she'd perfected came off beautifully. Five years and she could fake it with the best of them.

"Seriously, nothing's wrong. I'm watching movies with Jan."

"If something happens to you… Well, I'll just never forgive myself."

"Nothing will. Promise." She skipped down the hill, horrified at the lies she'd told.

One of the things she hadn't missed from her

old life was liars and users. People who had hung around her, claiming to be her friends, but who just wanted a free ride. They told her whatever lies were convenient. She'd let them and didn't care.

Not until four of them had died. One saving her life. Everything changed then.

Sissy really had died that night. She'd been a character invented out of necessity. Kylie was her real name. During those long days in the hospital, she had talked to herself in the mirror. Forcing her mind to reconnect to that real person.

Unable to attend the funerals of her friends… Scared that Xander would send someone to finish the job… Speaking only to her lawyer… She planned and prepared to run and hide. Leaving everything had been because of Xander. But leaving…that was all her idea.

She'd done it once when she'd signed on to become a model at the age of thirteen. Leaving the disaster of a life back then had been easy. Emancipation had been easy. Turning twenty-one and wheeling away from the hospital wasn't hard. It had saved her life. She was sure of it.

But today would be the hardest thing she'd ever done.

It didn't take long to catch up with the kids. "Hey slowpokes. I thought you'd be racing to get started. Once we finish this project, Bryce promised us all pizza."

"I what?"

"Pizza. Remember?" She caught up with him, looped her arm through his and the bag hanging over his shoulder. "You don't mind springing for pizza after all this hard work, do you? Or should I tell them that Rangers don't make enough money to buy three or four pies?"

"Pizza it is."

She broke apart from him, snagging her bag in the process. But she laughed and faked her way to the twisted trees. She plunged into the work, refusing to think of what was in store over the next few days.

Her map, compass, money and change of socks were with her. She'd had a moment of brilliance after Bryce had left. They'd be watching for her on every form of transportation. Xander might not know exactly how she looked now, but the people prosecuting his father did. They would trump up charges and arrest her. And he'd find her.

That was one thing she was certain about. There had already been one scandal this year about crooked state attorneys and politicians on the payroll of Paul Tenoreno.

"I don't know what you're planning, but you aren't going to shake me." Bryce walked up with a heavy-duty limb trimmer thingy.

"I have no idea what you're talking about." Her tree was ready to be cut. She signaled Martin who could handle the chain saw. She dug her earplugs out of her pocket. "Do you have ear pro-

tection? No? You might want to work on the next tree, then."

Bryce was angry. It showed in the way he chopped small limbs off and threw them into a pile. The kids then moved the brush to a larger pile that would be a bonfire later in the fall for their school. They worked. Hard.

Load after load of fireplace-size logs were added into a trailer that the ATV pulled up the hill. Richard was keeping track of how many were loaded by what team. Bryce was obviously in pain. Not from the physical labor—it was clear his muscles could handle that—it was the sunburn. His tight-fitting jeans didn't help much either. He'd switched from little limb lopping to splitting wood with an ax.

"If you guys moved about six feet, I think you'd be in the shade." She handed Bryce a bottle of water and lowered her voice, saying, "I think you could take off your shirt and stop rubbing your sunburn, too."

"You were right about my holster not being empty," he whispered back.

"I can stash it in my drawstring bag. It won't be out of your sight."

Did she have an ulterior motive? Not at first. She didn't want to steal his gun. But… No. She wouldn't steal his gun. Before she left, she'd hide

it in the barn. It would be out of sight and out of reach of the two granddaughters.

"You might as well put your phone in here, too." She blocked the view of him removing his weapon and placing it inside. "You can hear it if it rings."

That would be hidden, too. Hopefully it would slow him down not to have his phone.

"Wait." He shrugged out of his shirt. The light pink of that morning had turned a deep red. Small white spots—blisters—had formed from getting hot again. "The bag stays with me. You're moving around. I'm staying put."

Swinging the ax, he lodged it in a log and moved everything to the shade, taking her travel items and dropping them in his line of sight. Darn him. And it was almost time to go.

The last thing she wanted was to bring all these people into her problems. She couldn't create a diversion without a lot of repercussions. How was she going to get out of this? She shook her head as it came to her. It was the perfect excuse to head back to the house.

She finished up the last tree. The kids and parent volunteers had been great. The heat wasn't too bad since most of the area was still shaded. And in this little gully there was even a hint of a breeze.

I'm going to miss this so much.

But it was time to go.

No goodbyes. No tears. She set her tool near

the watercooler and stuffed her gloves in the back pocket of her shorts. She'd need them later. She waited, aware of where everyone was located. As soon as a couple of the boys brought another piece of a large trunk for Bryce to split, she took them all cups of water from the cooler.

"Drink up, boys. You need to stay hydrated."

"Thanks, Kylie," they said between sips.

"I'm heading to the little girls' room. So you fellows are on your own for a minute or two. Maybe even three." She smiled. The smile that teen boys had fallen for so many years ago. She casually bent and retrieved her bag.

"I can watch that for you." Bryce almost touched her arm but pulled it back to the ax handle. Probably remembering this morning's toss to the floor.

"I need what's inside. Understand?"

He nodded and those teenage boys sort of cringed. She giggled at her brilliance and waved to Richard for a lift.

The bathroom wasn't a bad idea. She grabbed a couple of apples from the kitchen counter, a soda and two bottles of water. She couldn't ask for them, so she left a five-dollar bill in the drawer.

With Bryce's gun and phone well-hidden inside the barn, she grabbed Little Bit and walked her to the far side of the house. There would be lots of sunlight left when she reached the north fence. If Bryce tried to follow her, he'd have to drive half

an hour to get to the road she was heading to that bordered the far side of the property.

She clicked to Little Bit and didn't look back as she loped away.

Chapter Four

Bryce mentioned he needed a break. Everyone was exhausted so Fred called out quitting time. They all walked up the incline while Fred and Richard rode in the ATV.

He had a very bad feeling why Kylie had been gone so long. His gut told him she'd left, along with his service weapon and his phone.

"Dammit."

"Something wrong?" Martin asked.

"Just slipped. These boots weren't made for climbing."

"Yeah, we noticed. But thanks for coming. You did a lot. You Kylie's boyfriend now or something?"

"No. I live across the street. I'm helping Mrs. Mackey out for a while." Might be longer if he'd lost his Sig to a runaway witness.

The kids gave each other fist bumps when they saw Mrs. Childers arrive with pizza boxes. It was

a familiar scene. He'd grown up in a small community. There was just one thing notably wrong… Kylie wasn't anywhere in sight.

For some reason, no one was overly concerned with her disappearance. That bugged him. Was he the only one not in on her planned escape? Did they already consider him the enemy?

The kids were sprawled across the porch cooling off. Proud of their work today, they were inhaling the pizza and soda. Richard and Fred were tallying the stacks of wood to determine which team won. Mrs. Childers and her granddaughters were bringing out cupcakes they'd made for the young people.

And Kylie was nowhere. Not in the house. Not waiting in the truck. Mrs. Childers shrugged and searched a little herself when he asked. Everywhere except the barn.

Still shirtless, because Kylie had taken that along with everything else, he cautiously walked through the barn's double doors. Open, clean, neat. If he hadn't been looking for something out of place, he'd never have caught the shirttail in the hayloft.

Wedged between a hay bale and the rafters, he pulled the shirt free and found his cell, badge and gun. Relief a hundred times over. No words could describe.

Since the gun was hidden, it meant that Kylie wasn't missing…just trying to disappear. Every-

thing in place and with his shirt on his back, he sought out Mrs. Childers for answers.

"Did you happen to drop Kylie off back in town?" He didn't want to seem overanxious, but his insides started to grind like coffee beans.

"Well, if I had, I would have told you when you were looking for her earlier." Lisa immediately turned her back to him but didn't walk away.

"Funny thing about honest folks trying to lie. They don't do it often enough to be good at it." He stood next to her and took the empty pizza boxes from her grip, setting them on the porch swing. "You may not have taken her back to town, but you know what's going on."

"No."

The worry in her eyes clued him in. She'd helped but had no details. "Mrs. Childers, I realize you're friends with Kylie and you have no reason to trust me. I need to show you something." He removed his badge and let her take a long look. "It's important that everyone in town not know who I work for."

"Then why tell me? Are you here to arrest Kylie? Because I won't help you."

"No, ma'am. It's worse. I'm here to protect her." Bryce put his badge away and leaned against the wall. He tried to be as casual as possible, attempting to gain any trust he could.

"If that's true, then why would she leave?" She

shook her head, one hand knotting in her apron still dusted with flour.

"She seems to be a very independent woman. Did you give her a ride?"

"No. And that's the truth. She's spending the night with Jan Turner and said she wanted to get to the northeast gate. The only way is on horseback. She said she'd leave the gear there and set Little Bit free. She wouldn't tell me anything else except that it was important for her to leave without anyone knowing. Is she in danger?"

"Thanks. You've helped tremendously." He took the porch steps two at a time.

"How are you going to find her?" Lisa asked behind him.

"With a lot of luck and crossed fingers."

No local PD involvement. At least not yet. He had to try to locate her on his own. Oh, yeah. He could follow tracks. He was a Texas Ranger who had a knack for computers. But at his roots, he was a simple country boy who'd grown up hunting with his dad.

"Richard?" Lisa shouted from the porch. "Will the four-wheeler get back to the northeast quarter of the property?"

"There's still too many downed trees," Richard replied.

"Well, then help Bryce saddle up Tinkerbell. He needs to save Kylie." Lisa's voice held a slight tremor of worry.

"Save Kylie?" Richard asked, but got an elbow in his ribs from Fred. "Whatever you say, dear."

Both men stopped what they were doing and moved to the barn. The one horse in the stall Bryce had seen earlier must be Tinkerbell.

He could approximate how long ago Kylie had left, but not how fast she could push the horse. There was also no way to know exactly how long it would take to catch up with her. The trees were thick in some parts and would make it hard to follow a trail.

"I can saddle her if you show me the tack," he told the men as they entered the barn. He wanted both of these guys to know he wasn't a novice.

"Doesn't make me no never mind." Richard mumbled and unlocked the storage room. "I've stayed married all these years by listening to Lisa. Doesn't make any sense riding a horse where you can drive. I just do what I'm told."

Fred snickered, clearly knowing something Bryce didn't. Then again…

"I appreciate the help, but aren't you guys curious as to *why* I need the horse?"

And there it was as plain as day turning to night. These honest men compressed their lips and dug the toes of their boots in the dirt.

"Did Mrs. Mackey tell you something about me?"

"Tell us what, son?" Fred asked as innocent as a five-year-old with his hand in a cookie jar.

"You know. And you want me on this horse pretty badly. In fact, I'd say you're practically throwing me on it." Bryce looked at the mare and had a bad feeling. "Give me your keys, Fred."

"What's that you're saying?" Fred held his hand, cupping his ear.

"Go ahead, Fred. He won't find her in the dark on his own and we're certainly not going to help him."

"I will not." The older man took a step back.

Richard looped the lead rope over the stall's gate and crossed his arms in defiance. "If we're lucky, he might be stuck out there all night and she'll get clean away."

Bryce opened his palm, taking a step closer.

Fred dug deep in his jeans pocket for the set of keys. He held them in a tight fist, not forking them over. "Maybe I should drive? That old motor gets kind of cranky."

"Thanks, but I think I'll get there faster on my own." Wherever *there* happened to be. "Pick it up at my place tomorrow."

Fred tossed. Bryce caught and hit the dirt running. Already tired, he should have been drinking a gallon of water to rehydrate. A slight headache had begun. Not to mention the idiot burn he had thanks to Jesse's suggestion of taking his shirt off.

He shifted the truck into High and skidded to a halt at the end of the long private driveway.

"Which way?"

His cell had no reception. No GPS. They might have counted on that. But he had the map he'd downloaded of the area. With details. Lots of details.

Kylie was headed to the northeast portion of Richard's property. Why would she go there? He enlarged the map and knew...there was no road that passed from US 281 on the west side of the Richard's place to County Road 238 on the east.

It would delay him to double back toward Hico and try to cut her off.

"Where will I find her?"

Had she made arrangements to be picked up on the country road? Was she just going to hoof it to the next town? It wasn't an impossible idea. But a faster way to disappear would be to hitch a ride. And if she walked the county roads northwest, she'd hit Highway 67 with plenty of traffic.

Everything rested with him making a logical guess.

He turned right instead of left back to town and pushed the truck harder than it had been pushed in a while. It sputtered a bit, but got the job done. The cooler air of twilight passed through the open windows. When he turned again, he could smell hay and cattle.

Working around Mrs. Mackey's house for the past couple of weeks had brought back a lot of

memories. The third time he'd called his mom, she'd asked him what was wrong and had kidded him about being homesick.

Homesick? He couldn't wait to leave his family's acreage and pass on his riding lawn mower duties to his younger brothers. They'd all left the house and were spread out across the country now, settled with families or kids on the way. He rested his elbow on the door and tapped a drum solo on the old-fashioned vent window.

Darkness was slowly growing. The moon wouldn't rise for quite a while so it might be harder to see someone walking in the fields. He'd taken the most direct route to the next county road Kylie might be on. He turned right again and kept the truck in second gear.

Reminiscing was fine, but his job was to find Kylie Scott. After he got her back to headquarters in Waco, he'd find out how Fred and Richard had known about his cover. The only person who supposedly knew was Mrs. Mackey. Why would she tell anyone?

It was dark enough that unless Kylie had a flashlight, he wouldn't be able to see her. He continued along the road at a normal pace for the truck. How would he explain this wild situation to Major Parker?

If she disappeared again on his watch, he might not have to explain anything to anyone.

THE DAY HAD already been long and exhausting before Kylie had started traipsing through uneven fields in her tennis shoes. She couldn't rush. There was no flashlight or even a penlight in her bag. And it was just her luck that tonight there wasn't even a moon.

Hours after leaving the horse, her legs were cramping and she was thirstier than she'd ever been. And hot. There was no breeze to cool the sweat that dripped in buckets down her back. She'd pulled her color contacts and stowed them in her bag.

She'd avoided the roads, but kept them just to her left. No one had driven past her. Or at least she hadn't heard any vehicles. The birds she'd come across had practically scared her senseless.

Each time she'd carefully squeezed between the strands of wire fence from one field to the other, her fingers were crossed that there wouldn't be a bull or something more dangerous in her path. She pulled herself through the last pieces of barbed wire fencing and picked up her bag, straightening and stretching her back.

The hardest part of the hike was done. She could follow this road to the closest thing this area had to a highway—a two-lane blacktop. Then all she had to do was hitch a ride and she was...

She was what?

The word *free* kept trying to finish the sentence. But she wasn't free. If she was free to

choose where she wanted to live, it would be Hico. She'd never felt more at home in a community. They accepted that she didn't talk about her time before living there. They really didn't know anything about her.

At least not the *previous* her. The Sissy Jorgenson her. Such a fake. It had taken a while, but Sissy had been laid to rest with all the cool kids she'd hung out with.

Unfortunately, Sissy wouldn't have had anything to do with Kylie Scott. And she wouldn't have waited two weeks to have a fling with the guy across the street. One look at his body and Sissy would have been all over him.

Bryce was nice looking. He was also a Texas Ranger ready to take her back to Austin whether she liked it or not. It didn't matter if she knew about the Tenoreno family business. The attorneys five years ago had offered her protection in exchange for information.

Did they really think she would have walked away so quickly if she'd known enough to put those men behind bars?

Blinding headlights popped on in front of her.

"I was just coming to look for you." Bryce's voice came from next to Fred's truck. "You going to run again?"

"Mind shutting off the floodlights?" Kylie saw his silhouette lean through the window and everything got dark again.

With no place to go and no energy to run, she accepted the setback, but not defeat. Somehow, she'd get away from Bryce Johnson and get on with another new start.

"Want a ride?" he asked with an air of innocence.

"Yes, if you're heading back to Hico."

"It's on the way to Waco." He casually leaned against Fred's pickup.

"How long have you been waiting?"

"At least an hour." Bryce tapped the old green truck. "Did the horse throw you or something during your evening ride? Get turned around finding your friend's house or the way back? I know you weren't attempting to run away. Right?"

She didn't need to answer. He was making fun of her so she glared at him, even though he couldn't see the glare in the dark. She wrapped her arms around her bag, almost afraid he might arrest her on the spot.

"Are you as starved as me? Or did Lisa give you something before you left?" Bryce continued, fingers tapping out an unknown rhythm against the old metal truck.

"I'm actually starved. And parched. Any chance there's a water bottle in there?" She leaned on the warm hood.

"Nope. But it's not far to Hico." He threw his thumb toward the cab. "We can get something to go."

"Nothing is open at this time of night in our little town." The sun had been down a long time. Too long for the hood to still be as warm as it was. "You must be a really lucky son of a gun to choose the exact road I was heading to."

"I like to think of myself as a highly skilled Texas Ranger. Come on, get in."

"Who had his gun and ID lifted by little ol' me," she mumbled.

"There's no reason to get nasty."

"I'll admit defeat when you confess how you found me."

"I had a map. Calculated your foot speed—they teach us things like that."

"And how long have you really been here?"

"All right. I tried several roads before deciding on this one. Satisfied? I got lucky and saw something moving from the road over there. Been waiting about fifteen minutes."

"So you guessed."

"Pretty much." He grinned.

The dark wasn't pitch-black, even with no moon hanging overhead. She could see that he'd found his shirt from where she'd hidden it in the barn. That meant he'd found his gun, too. Bryce could force her to go with him. If he was a dirty cop he could make her disappear. Especially now that she'd told Lisa she had to leave town.

No one would be looking for her.

There was nothing she could do to prevent it.

Not here. She had to get back to town, maybe show her face at the Stop-N-Get It. But her instincts told her that Bryce was legit. A good person who believed he was following the law and had her best interests at heart.

Right. That's what they all say.

"If I keep walking down this road…" She threw her chin in the direction behind the truck. "Are you going to arrest me?"

"Don't make me, Kylie."

Her fingers were already wrapped around the handle. She was getting into the truck, she had little choice. But she didn't have to like it. They both got inside and slammed their doors.

"You need someone to look out for your safety," he said softly, reaching for the ignition key.

"No offense, but I think I was doing pretty good without you."

Exhaustion like she hadn't felt in five years hit her like a slow wave as soon as she sat down. It started in her shoulders and crept up her neck, then down her back. She hadn't stopped and had barely slowed, holding a steady pace across those fields. And yet, Texas Ranger Bryce Johnson had been waiting on her.

Just dumb luck? Or was he really that skilled?

Chapter Five

As soon as Bryce had put the truck in gear, Kylie's head sank against the window and she was asleep. Totally and deeply. The mumbles and sleep jerking couldn't be faked. Not that well. A little twitch, then a jerk that should have awakened anyone who was dozing.

Exhaustion had overtaken her. He'd probably have to carry her inside her house when they arrived. As long as there weren't any alarms. *Get a grip.* They weren't staying.

A quick stop to grab water and clothes. That was it. He was taking her to Waco. Tonight. No waiting. No discussion.

The truck was much too noisy to hear the sleepy words escaping her lips. He couldn't see her face, but could imagine the soft worried crease across her forehead. He'd watched her all afternoon. Had suspected that she was up to something

and should never have let her leave—especially with his gun.

But for some reason he'd trusted her to realize how much danger she was in. Maybe that was the problem. Maybe she knew and didn't expect him to be able to protect her from the Tenoreno family. He could understand that.

Sort of.

Running had been a logical choice. She didn't know him. He had to respect that she'd had a plan. Been prepared. Five years after she'd disappeared and she'd still been ready to take off with nothing. Smart.

Then again, she'd left his weapon behind.

Crazy woman.

Maybe smarter than he'd been thinking about her for the past three years. Smarter than Sissy Jorgenson had been when she married Xander. Kylie Scott was a completely different person, who didn't mind working hard side by side with teens who needed some guidance.

Why? What had changed her? Besides the near death experience, of course.

They were almost back to town when she mumbled something about getting down. Her head tossed back and forth in a bad dream. Her long legs kicked out, striking the metal of the truck near her feet.

Kylie jerked awake. She looked frantically all around her. "Oh my gosh. We're not home yet?"

"Bad dream?"

"Let's just say that for a short one, it was really intense." She dropped her window farther and dipped her hand in the wind blowing past the mirror. "I wish the Koffee Cup was open this late. I sure could go for some pie."

"The fresh strawberry was really good this morning."

"This morning? You had pie for breakfast?" Her hand fluttered to the door handle.

"Fruit is good for you." He slowed the truck to a stop, very aware that there'd be no way he could stop her from jumping from the old vehicle. She might get a head start, but he'd catch her. She might know her way around town better, but she was also more tired than he was.

"How do you eat pie for breakfast and look that good?" She shook her head. "Never mind. It's a guy thing. I get it."

"A guy thing?" He loved the blue flash of her eyes, even if the look was a little deadly. He really wanted to ask about the "looking good" statement. Maybe the sunburn was worth it after all.

The light turned green and her elbow rested on the window's edge again. He liked the way this woman's brain worked. She was constantly ready. Had distracted him with the pie conversation, yet had thought her choices through before acting rash and running.

"Where are you going? Our street is to your left."

"Yeah, I know." He took a second right into the motel nearest the highway. One car in the parking lot. Sliding the camera app open, he handed Kylie his phone. "Can you snap the license?"

"Sure," she whispered like someone inside the room could hear them. "You sure this is legal?"

"Very. It will give me a heads-up if anyone's here that might be looking for you."

He swung around and they repeated the picture-taking at the other two hotels in town. She was out of the truck before he pulled to a complete stop once they were in front of her house.

"Kylie, wait." He pulled the key and caught up before she opened her front door. He stopped her hand on the knob. "I need to check it out first."

"Go ahead. Where do you want me to wait? Here on the porch all alone? Or just inside where the bogeyman can sneak up on me? Or, I know, out in the woods where the ax murderer is sure to be waiting?"

"The woods are out?" Humor or sarcasm... probably not the best way to handle the situation. Truth it was. "Hand on my shoulder. I go. You go. I stop. You stop. Stay close behind me until we check all the rooms. Got it?"

"Sure." She shook her head and placed her hand on his shoulder with a firm grip.

He drew his Sig and entered the house. If someone was inside, they'd just given them time to se-

cure their position and prepare to overpower them. It was a chance they'd take.

"Stop." She tapped his shoulder. "Alarm." She pushed the code and the light turned green.

Bryce had a feeling that Kylie wouldn't be satisfied just getting a glass of water. He also planned to find her gun of choice that was stowed in the bathroom before she did.

Slowly, he checked out each of the rooms in the small home. One uncomfortable couch, one compact kitchen, two bedrooms, one bed and an empty bath.

"Does it look like anyone's been here?"

"No. Excuse me a minute." She pushed on his shoulder to get him to move.

"Not yet. We need to look in the garage."

"Seriously? My eyeballs are floating."

He resisted laughing and managed to question her with a look. Taking her hand, he placed it back on his shoulder and kept his over it until they were back down the hall and he found the door locked.

"But—"

"Shh. Where's the key?" Not just a dead bolt to turn. He'd assumed that it was extra protection when he'd seen the security lock that morning. Now, with her hesitation, he wasn't that sure.

"It hasn't been messed with so there's no reason to go in there."

"I need to be certain, Kylie."

She stared at him a second. Placed her hands

on her hips the next. Then reluctantly pulled open a cabinet drawer without looking. Inside was a small combination box. She rolled the numbers and dangled a set of keys from her fingertips.

"You're going to want to know the whole story behind this and I'm not ready to share it. So can you check out the garage and forget about it for tonight?" He reached for the keys and she yanked them back. "Your word, Ranger Johnson."

"That's asking a lot from a guy here to protect you."

"That remains to be seen." She tossed the key ring, crossed her arms and released an exaggerated sigh.

Bryce opened the door and cautiously stepped down to the garage level. Kylie flipped the light switch causing him to blink. A single set of shelves across from him held some labeled boxes. Christmas decorations, patriotic, miscellaneous, fall theme, Halloween and one that was unmarked.

But taking up all the room in the single car garage was a vehicle covered with sheets. The sheets across the trunk had a layer of dust on them. Unlike the one in front. No one had disturbed anything anywhere in the house, including here.

But he was curious. He holstered his Sig and tugged, letting the sheets slide to a pile at his boots.

In the time that he'd been watching her, Kylie had ridden a bike to work, walked to the store or

caught a ride. He'd never seen a car unless someone else was picking her up like today. So the beauty in the garage was a surprise.

"Where did you get this?"

"We can't take it anywhere. It's stolen."

"Can I ask why you kept it then?" He slid his hand along the stylish fin from the '60s and immediately regretted spoiling the clean shine.

"I didn't want that louse to have it." She threw up her hands. "All right. I admit it. I sort of took it to get back at him. I was so angry that he'd taken everything from me that I wanted something of his that he'd miss."

"This belonged to Xander Tenoreno?" The black Cadillac had a fire-engine red interior and was in mint condition. The paint job was still shiny and bright. He stroked the edge as he walked to the front of the garage.

If Kylie hadn't touched the car, someone had. There was a battery charger near the tire. So he could no longer assume she didn't have a vehicle to drive. He'd bet money that this one would move pretty good.

"Of course it did. Does." She walked to the opposite side of the car, but leaned against the unfinished wall with her hands behind her. "I left the hospital when I knew the family was gone. I wanted my stuff. Anything really. Or maybe some cash to get out of the country. I used what little I had to bribe one of the guards to let me in. The

bastard had moved everything. Even the cat. It was like I'd never existed."

"So you grabbed his car?"

"One of them."

"This one's pretty distinctive."

"I know. It was new so I figured it would be missed. I didn't say I was thinking straight at the time. I drove until I ran out of gas."

"To Hico? That's how you got here? How you chose this town to hide out?"

"Not very strategic, right? This gas guzzler coasted to a stop right next to the Billy the Kid statue. The top was down and I put the seat back. I stared at that statue and fell asleep. Fred drove by the next morning and helped me push the car to the station."

"So he talked you into staying?"

"He took me to breakfast. Denise just had a baby and Allison offered me a temporary job right there on the spot. I'm sure Fred had something to do with it. He almost always does."

"If the engine is in good condition, I'm surprised you haven't tried to sell it."

"You heard me say it's stolen, right? It seems so simple in my head—drive the car and I get killed. There isn't a different version. Xander would know I've been living here if this car was discovered."

"Lots of stolen cars are illegally traded. You

probably could have gotten enough money to leave town. So why did you stay?"

Why run? He knew that the state's attorney had offered her immunity for anything connected with illegal activity. All she had to do was give them evidence. Anything to help break up the Teno-reno family's crime syndicate. Instead she'd stolen a car.

"If my ex-husband didn't already want me dead, knowing that I've had his precious car all this time would be another reason to hunt me down. It makes me nervous to even look at it. I haven't glanced at it in at least two years. Fred keeps it polished." She reached for the corner of the sheet. "And I stayed in Hico because I like it here."

"You most likely had it off the streets before it was reported missing. We might be able to lay out a trap using it as bait if he loved it as much as you say." He slid his hand over the polished tailfin again. "Man, I'd love to take it for a spin."

"What is it with guys and cars? It's not going anywhere." She dragged the dusty cover over the trunk. "Taking it brought me to Hico, but driving it now will just get us killed."

He grabbed the opposite corner and helped hide the convertible. "We'll take my truck to Waco. I was thinking about later. After you're safe."

"There isn't a later. Don't you get it? I won't be safe. Ever. If I go with you, Xander *will* find me. He's probably already sent someone. Just let me

go." She draped the hood and crossed her arms, protecting herself. "You could tell everyone you didn't pick the right road to wait at. It might be a little embarrassing, but we'd both be alive."

"I CAN'T DO THAT, KYLIE."

She wanted to be relaxed, cool, act as if none of this conversation bothered her. It did. Thinking about Xander and the men he had working for him bothered her a lot.

Bryce lifted his arm, waiting on her to pass through the garage entrance to her kitchen. She didn't like the feeling of helplessness. It made her mad. There was nothing in the kitchen to help her overpower this man. Her aikido skills had paid off this morning, but he was prepared for them now. She couldn't outrun him to the bathroom and she couldn't lock him in the garage since he had the door behind him waiting on her.

So she passed in front of him and stepped onto her worn linoleum. He'd already mentioned that he thought she had a gun stashed in the bathroom. If she asked to go, he was the kind of guy who would search it thoroughly beforehand. He might even find it.

"Want a bottle of water?" she asked.

"Been craving something cold for the past hour." Bryce wiped the sweat from his forehead. "But water will do."

"Yeah, I know what you mean." She went to the

fridge and grabbed two bottles, tossing one across the room to him as he locked the door. It didn't escape her that the keys to the Cadillac dropped into his pocket.

They both stayed put in the dark and drank their bottles dry. Bryce crunched his to a fistful of plastic and set it on the table. Sixteen ounces of fluid didn't seem to be enough for her thirst so she opened the fridge for more.

"Kylie!"

Bryce dived across the open section of kitchen, knocking her to the floor behind him and dragging her to the far side of the refrigerator.

The window shattered. Milk streamed across the floor toward them. Orange juice exploded sending glass in the opposite direction.

"You okay?" he asked, pulling her around the wall into the living room. "Thank God I saw their sighting laser."

He pulled his weapon but as soon as he stuck his head around the corner things in the kitchen began shattering again.

"Call 911," he shouted.

"No, I won't. These men will kill responding officers without blinking an eye." She was crazy for thinking they could take care of this themselves. His look told her as much, but she didn't want anyone to get hurt trying to save her. "Too many have already died."

He took out his cell and in a quick call told

whoever answered what their situation was. "They've got us pinned down." Backup was on its way. "The thickness of the refrigerator on the other side of this wall is the only thing protecting us. Don't move until I come up with a plan."

Her life wasn't worth more than anyone else's. She had to do something. If someone got shot, how would she live with that again? The white gravel lot had been drenched in blood. She barely remembered shooting details and yet, the image was so vivid.

Red on white. Just like Darren lying on top of her.

As much as she hated the memories, she clung to them to remind herself. She wouldn't forget how vicious Xander was or how he didn't value human life. Everything was different…except that.

Bryce had his arm across her chest. She was loosely pinned to the wall where he'd leaned just that morning for support. Something—maybe a clay pot one of the rec center kids had given her—exploded in front of them.

A couple of choice words escaped from Bryce. "Dammit. They've shot a hole through the damn wall. What caliber are they using? When our backup gets here…"

She was paralyzed in place, hearing only half of what he instructed. She caught on to the fact

he wanted her to slide her head to the floor and lie flat.

"Kylie? Can you hear me? Understand what I'm explaining?"

"I can…I can do it. But why?"

"Their next approach should be coming through the front. It's wood and glass—easy enough to penetrate with the firepower they have." He bobbed his head when the television screen was pierced by another bullet.

"You're coming, too?"

"I might be on top of you if you're too slow." Bryce extended his legs and pushed her couch across the old wood floor.

A small coffee table blocked a clean path to the door, but she could get around it. She wasn't paralyzed any longer. "Are you sure we shouldn't just get up and run?"

Something glass exploded into a gazillion pieces. She covered her eyes. She didn't want to think it, but it looked like someone had shot through the front door.

Bryce answered his phone. "Johnson. From the southwest. No visual on the north. We're pinned in the front room. Got it." He stowed the phone and covered most of her body. "We're staying put. Three police cars are en route."

"Call them off, Bryce. Please. They'll be slaughtered." She turned to her side. His arm was wrapped around her waist. She tried to scoot

away, but he pulled her back to him. She shoved at his chest and he captured her hand.

"We aren't going anywhere and the officers are doing their jobs. They aren't coming in blind. They can handle the shooter. We'll be fine." He patted her back.

Was he shushing her? He pulled her face to his shirt when something else burst behind her. He smelled musky. The good kind after working all day. She could feel the heat from his sunburn through the soft cotton. It was comforting, even if she didn't want to admit that it had been a long time since she'd been held by a man. Or anyone.

But she couldn't let herself be comfortable. She stretched her neck backward so she could look him in the eye and tell him what he could do with his "shushing."

Glass rained around them as the front windows shattered above their heads. Xander's men weren't leaving anything to chance. She waited for the bullet to pierce her skin.

For the second time she knew her life was over.

Chapter Six

Shots were fired outside the house. A multitude of ear-piercing pops. Some single rounds like at the gun range. Some rapid like five years ago. Would the men who had them pinned here run? Could the cops actually scare them away?

Lying there, waiting to be shot, Bryce had rolled her to her belly and shielded Kylie from the shards. The weight of the man on top of her should have kept her from breathing easily. He'd supported most of his weight on his arms to keep from hurting her. It took her a couple of seconds of silence to realize he wasn't moving, but it wasn't the weight of the dead like Darren.

Bryce was still breathing. There was a gap between his arm and the floor where she could see parts of her living room. Or what used to be her living room—war zone was more accurate.

A beam of light broke the semidarkness.

She wasn't in a hurry to be free. She needed to

catch her breath and get back to the present. This wasn't a white gravel parking lot. She hadn't been shot. They were alive.

"Police! Johnson? Kylie? You in here?"

She recognized the voice. She'd stood next to Todd Harris at the Chamber of Commerce pancake breakfast last year. He'd told her all about his three kids, especially his son who had hit a rebellious period.

That's how and when Martin Harris had gotten involved in their teen program. He was one of the leaders now. She was proud to have helped that father and teen. And now he was putting his life in danger for her.

"I'm okay." She waited for Bryce to roll. He was slow but finally moved to his side.

"Is the perimeter secure?" He groaned.

"We're working on it," Todd said. "You good here? You shot? Need an ambulance?"

"You're bleeding?" Kylie carefully put her knees in the glass-free zone where her body had been during the attack. She watched Bryce sit, awkwardly limiting his movements.

Todd turned his flashlight behind them drawing her attention. "What the hell did they shoot at you? A cannon?"

The hole in her wall next to where they'd been sitting was indeed the size of a cannonball. Whatever it had been, she was glad the old refrigerator had enough thickness to protect them.

"Sure felt like it. We're good. I got us covered." Bryce seemed a little out of breath as he spoke. "Can you watch the perimeter of the house? We need ten minutes."

"Not a problem," Todd answered and picked his way back to the door.

Afraid that another round of shots would happen at any minute, she kept her eyes on Todd and possible movement behind him. Of course the only light was from the porch across the street. Not much help at all.

"Do you know who did this or think they'll come back?" Todd asked, plainly wanting the Texas Ranger to issue the orders.

"My guess is they didn't want us dead," Bryce answered out of breath. "Otherwise, they would have rushed the house. They'll wait for a second attempt when they can grab whatever they're really after. Might already be out of town."

"Well," Todd drawled, "it won't hurt to look."

Bryce sucked air through his teeth catching Kylie's attention. She turned and caught him pulling a large piece of glass from his forearm.

"Are you crazy?" She slapped his hand away. "Let me get a first aid kit. If they're too deep, you'll need a doctor."

He clapped a hand on her arm. "I'll go with you."

They helped each other stand. He didn't let go of her while he addressed Todd, giving him in-

structions on how far to set up checkpoints. She'd had no intention to get her hidden handgun, but evidently he hadn't forgotten about it.

Nor did he trust her to leave it there. The glass was lodged mainly in his left arm. He shook off some pieces stuck in the fine arm hair before they left the room.

"Everything's gone. Completely destroyed." There really was nothing left of her cute little home. The curtains were in shreds, everything was cut in half or shattered on the floor.

"We're alive."

"For now," she whispered.

He sat on the toilet lid, covered in a red faux fur that she adored. She went straight to the cabinet, keeping her eyes away from the picture on the wall. Tweezers, alcohol, Band-Aids…she laid everything side by side on the short counter.

"You've certainly been through the wringer today." She took a good look under the bright light.

"These are just scratches, but a couple do look like they need tweezers."

"You should be plenty sore from the sunburn and swinging that ax." She pulled the rod that held the stopper in place. "Hold your arm over the sink."

Bryce did as he was told, hissing as she poured the alcohol across his skin. It had to burn, but he didn't wave at it. She thought about blowing on

his skin, but it seemed too intimate. So she poured more alcohol over the tweezers and went to work picking out the shards.

"The Hico police turned out to be more competent than you gave them credit." Bryce winced. "Are you surprised that we're all still alive?"

"What about the next time? Who's going to get hurt then?"

"I'm taking you to Waco and if anyone's watching they'll know it. Then they'll be facing a company of Rangers."

"Or not." She placed the last bandage over the deepest cut, then wrapped his forearm with gauze.

"Why do you keep saying that? Don't you want to get to safety?"

"Of course I do, but I've tried explaining this not only to you but to everyone I spoke with five years ago. I simply don't know anything. I don't have anything worth trading for protection." She backed away from the sink. Thinking over and over again that she shouldn't look anywhere else in the bathroom. She needed to stare at Bryce and forget about taking the gun.

"Would you like some more aloe?" she asked, remembering the warmth of his skin. She put the kit away and grabbed a tube of cream, making the decision for him. "Take off your shirt."

He stood. The bathroom shrank. The result was like washing a cashmere sweater in a hot load of whites.

"Thanks for the offer, but I need to check on our rescue team."

They switched places, hands their only barrier between bodies sliding next to each other. "I really need a drink."

"Not a bad idea." Bryce rested his wrists on top of her shoulders. "Something stronger than water this round?"

"I don't think they shot the top shelf of the pantry. There's probably still a bottle intact." Tilting her face in his direction required as much bravery as sitting petrified while bullets were shot through her walls. "That is, if you're serious."

Bryce tapped her shoulder a couple of times, made eye contact, looked away, then back again. She had a good view of his Adam's apple jumping up and down as he swallowed hard. He was nervous. Because of her? Or was it because there was barely anything left of her house?

"We should…um…wait for another time. As much as I'd love a shot of whatever you have, I need to get you out of here. No way to secure—you know…" He squinted as he looked down the hall.

"Is there something you want, Bryce? I thought you were going to check on Todd."

"Is that his name?" He nodded his head as if agreeing with her. His lips were compressed in a straight line, but still looked inviting.

Honestly, they could have been standing on her

porch waiting to say good-night. The moment felt more like that than of ten minutes after someone had tried to kill them. Maybe she was in shock. Maybe she was just tired of fighting the inevitable.

Or maybe in spite of the weird circumstances that had brought them together, Bryce was as attracted to her as she was to him. Maybe. If she was lucky.

She cleared her throat and gently slid his hands from her shoulders. "Todd Harris, father of three teenagers all rooting for rival Texas colleges every Saturday afternoon. He mostly works weeknights now so his wife, Irma, could take the day shift. She's a nurse in Stephenville."

"Sounds like a nice family."

"And I want to keep it that way. Those kids need their father. Don't order him to—"

"Todd Harris has a job to do, Kylie. He signed up for this." Bryce tried to look stern. It didn't work on him.

"Get real. He signed up to make sure people drove the speed limit and to get cats out of little old ladies' trees."

"I think you might need that drink more than you think." He backed his wide shoulders through the doorway and latched on to her hand. "On the rocks or straight?"

"Can I get some clothes? My toothbrush?"

He pulled her into the kitchen. There was a

more concentrated destruction path. Her refrigerator was completely ruined. Her free hand began shaking and she couldn't stop it.

The mess was surreal. It registered on levels she didn't—couldn't—comprehend. She did need a drink. Perhaps more than one. But she *hadn't*. Not in five years.

"This is some good stuff." Bryce grabbed the whiskey from the top shelf. Then took a tumbler from the drain.

The bottle was half-gone. He unscrewed the cap, tipped the bottle...

"Wait. I can't. Especially that stuff." She shook her head, matching her hands. "It was in the car, Bryce. It belonged to...to Xander. I don't drink anymore. Can we just go?"

That bottle was a symbol of her past life. It and the car were the only two things she'd kept.

"Sure. I'll grab your toothbrush."

She turned looking at the broken things she'd collected. "Forget it. I need a new one anyway."

The clothes, things, books and even the house would be easy to leave behind. She picked up one of the photos that had been held in place by magnets on her ruined fridge. Fred and Lisa had locked her in the jail in the museum.

"It was a bet about how tall I was." She flipped the milk-drenched photo toward Bryce. "You see, Lisa thought I was over six feet and that's how

tall the old cell is. So when I stood inside…she thought she'd won. I didn't point out that my shoes had heels."

Tears. It had been a very long time since she'd cried over the life she'd given up.

Bryce used a scraped knuckle to wipe the trail dry. "You'll see your friends again, Kylie. I promise."

"It's out of your control. You can't keep a promise like that." More scared than she'd been in a while, she could barely whisper.

"She'll see her friends right now."

FRED SNELL HAD marched through the debris, crunching glass, not attempting to be quiet. Bryce hadn't heard a thing. Admittedly, his ears were still ringing from the gunshots. But his focus had been on Kylie instead of on keeping her safe.

"I would have gotten here sooner, but someone hijacked my truck. I had to call Bernie for a lift." Fred angled his back to Bryce and took Kylie in his arms.

"I'll call the officers for an escort to my truck and out of town." Bryce had his phone in hand about to hit Redial.

There was something about the look that Fred shot him. Anger. Disbelief. Defiance. The emotions of a protective father.

"Is that what *you* want, Kylie?" Fred asked, already assuming he knew she didn't.

"I don't seem to have a say in the matter. Fred, Bryce is a Texas Ranger."

"I know."

"I told them this afternoon." But they'd already known.

"I knew before that, son."

"Does everybody in this entire town already know?"

"Probably. Most of them are standing out in the yard waiting to find out what happened here. It's not too often that we have a shoot-out on Pecan Street." Fred crossed to a still-shaking Kylie and hugged her with one arm. "I think you two can use some pie."

"The Koffee Cup is closed."

"Don't mind that little detail. I know the owner." Fred secured Kylie with an arm around her shoulders. His lanky frame was a bit deceptive considering how he'd worked all afternoon. "We'll take my old Chevy and Ranger Johnson there can grab his newfangled vehicle after he straightens out this mess."

"Fred, I can't allow that."

"It's Ranger Snell, retired. She'll be all right, son. I've got a couple of men already on their way to keep her safe."

"There's no way she can stay here."

"Are you arresting her, Bryce?"

"That wasn't the plan."

"Then do what you have to do and know she's safe."

"No, sir." Bryce stopped the older man as he tried to leave. "She stays with me. I think we could both use some coffee, but it'll be at my house. I'm under orders. She's not leaving my sight."

"Good for you, Ranger. Good for you." Fred patted his hand against Bryce's chest. "We're agreed that she needs to leave?"

"Yes, sir. I just need to find Officer Harris."

"He's trying to get people to head home." Fred guided her into the living room. "Come on, sweetie."

"Bryce?"

"Want that toothbrush?" He winked, trying to let her know that everything would be okay.

Nodding to Fred to move ahead of him, he drew his weapon and followed steps behind Kylie. There was a crowd of about forty gathered in front of the house. He looked around and didn't see any unusual people. Most were couples or men he'd seen driving rigs and parking at their homes.

A retired Texas Ranger. Hard of hearing Fred. Who would have thought that? Mrs. Mackey might have told Fred about who was living in her house as soon as Company F had put the plan into motion. Just his luck that his first field operation had turned into such a disaster.

This wasn't all about him, though. His assign-

ment was about Kylie's safety. Her insistence that she didn't know anything was a problem. Whatever she knew, whatever she had on Xander Tenoreno it had to be big.

Something had kept them alive through that shoot fest. He had no illusions that he'd done anything to keep them safe. He'd walked them right into a death trap.

Whoever had been firing at them had taken their time and what? Deliberately missed?

The big question was why.

Chapter Seven

"Eventually the police will begin a search. They will find you and where will I be? Back at the beginning. The girl will get away and I won't have leverage." Daniel Rosco felt his body tense with the anger pulsing through him. "I have waited five years for this freedom. Do not rob me of it!"

Daniel threw the cell across the room. He didn't care that it burst apart. The burner wouldn't be used again. The dent in the wall might be noticed by his wife's maid, but was easily explained away with a lie.

"They had her, Papa. The incompetents had her and wasted our element of surprise." He spoke to a picture on the mantel. His father and mother had both been executed by the Tenorenos. "I swear on your graves that those bastards will not get away with this."

"Daniel, are you all right? I thought I heard something fall?" Nancy peeked through the door

connecting their rooms before coming through wearing nothing but her dressing gown. "Whatever's happened, it will be okay, sweetheart. Do you want to talk about it instead of ruining the paintings?"

She wrapped her arms around him, flattening her breasts against his back. The comforting hug was not enough to assuage his anger.

"I apologized for the Rivera and have replaced it."

"Darling, that's not the point. I don't like to see you this upset." She rubbed her hands up and down his chest. "Sit on the bed and let me help get rid of all this tension."

He covered one of her hands and brought it to his lips. "You're good to me. But this tension is good. It keeps me on edge."

"It's going to send you to an early grave. What went wrong? Didn't they find where Sissy Jorgenson was hiding?"

"Yes. But a cop is with her now. He saved her life and called the local PD."

"I can understand your frustration about them not completing their job, but you must be happy that the information we paid for is solid. Xander has been hiding her all these years. That tells us she must mean something to him."

"We've lost the element of surprise. They'll be watching for the men and more prepared to fend

them off. I've been lying low long enough. It's time to reclaim my heritage."

He spun Nancy in his arms and kissed her hard, pushing open her robe and feeling the artificial breasts she admired so much. He used the frustration he felt to have sex, bending her over the lounge chair. She didn't complain. She'd rather spend their time coupling than talking. It was the real reason she'd come into the room and they both knew it.

Afterward, he carried her to bed, lighting them both cigarettes and pouring his favorite whiskey three fingers deep into two glasses. He'd need it if he was going to take her again. She expected it. He hated that she did and would get what she wanted.

She was propped against the headboard with the pillows behind her. He left the cigarette to burn in the ashtray and threw the whiskey back so it would burn sliding down his throat. Then he lay face down across his wife's legs, allowing her to drag her nails across his skin.

The action soothed him anyway. It was a familiar routine. An action that needed no words. Familiarity that kept him just far enough from the edge that he wouldn't lose it.

He thought of Xander and how much he hated him.

"Daniel, stop. You need to relax, love. Focus on the good. We're close. So close," she whispered.

"This setback is a little bump in the road. We'll get our revenge. Don't doubt that."

He controlled his body, keeping it slack. But he let his mind list the ways he would destroy Xander with the retrieval of the flash drive. He'd tease him first with the knowledge someone had betrayed him.

It wasn't enough to kill Xander's ex-wife. He wanted Xander to cry out in pain. To suffer. And Daniel wanted to watch the Tenoreno family fall.

Then—and only then—he'd tell Xander why.

Chapter Eight

Bryce and his self-appointed armed partner cleared the rented house. First phone call was to Officer Harris who moved his three officers closer for a protection detail spanning both houses. The officers hadn't spoken to anyone who had spotted the shooters. After this much time it wasn't likely they'd find anything in the dark.

While the coffee brewed, his second phone call had been to Major Parker. To say the man was unhappy was an understatement. He also verified that Fred had served a distinguished career in Company A before he retired. Backup was on its way. Jesse had texted five minutes ago that he'd been ordered to lend assistance.

He'd be lucky if Jesse hadn't sent a mass email letting the rest of the state know he was coming to Bryce's rescue.

The house was secure. Kylie hadn't been out of his sight. Fred had been standing next to her

the entire time. They'd said very few words. The older man watched the backyard and occasionally squeezed her shoulder. The comforting seemed to help her to be patient.

Time for some answers.

"Before you get yourself all worked up..." Fred pulled out a dining room chair, joining Kylie at the table. "I recognized you, Johnson, as soon as you got to town. I read the news and keep up with current events. So no one informed me that you were here. Even without your glasses it would be hard to miss one of the Rangers who helped bring down Paul Tenoreno last spring."

"Why the interest in Kylie? Why do you want to keep her in town?"

"She's our friend and hasn't done anything wrong. It's not a question about keeping her. If she wants to leave, then she can leave."

"Fred," Kylie began, "there's something you should know."

"That you used to be married to a Tenoreno or that he tried to kill you five years ago? I recognized you when you ran out of gas. Hard not to. Everyone thought you'd been abducted and murdered. Your face was all over the news, honey." Fred scratched the white stubble on his chin. "This ain't my first rodeo. I was in law enforcement my entire life. Took me a bit longer to reach Texas Ranger than you, kid. Loved every minute of it

once I did. It's not like you just stop because you ain't wearing the badge."

"You never said a word." Kylie looked completely astonished.

"Neither did you." Fred winked and grinned. The old man was having a blast. "We all figured that when you were ready, you'd tell us. After a couple of years, we figured it was better for you if you didn't talk about it."

"Who all knows her real identity?" They both ignored Bryce, continuing their own conversation.

"I can't believe you did all that for me. I was so lost. If it hadn't been for you and Allison at the Koffee Cup, I would have been... Fred, I don't know what would have happened to me."

"You settled in here real good, young lady. We wanted to keep you." The smile on Fred's face was as genuine as his words.

"This is all very inspiring," Bryce interrupted, "but it still doesn't solve our problem or answer my question. I've been ordered to bring Kylie to Austin for questioning by the state attorneys."

"Then I'd like to see the warrant or summons. Sorry, son, but if Kylie doesn't want to go...she's not going."

"We're just talking for now. Nobody wants to issue a warrant, especially if Kylie hasn't done anything wrong." He tried to catch her gaze. He didn't want everyone to know Tenoreno's stolen car sat in her garage. Hell, maybe everyone in

Hico already knew. "I need a list of people who know who Kylie is and what happened to her before she arrived five years ago."

"Most everybody thinks of Kylie as someone who the community took in and who gives back to us a hundredfold. Few know that a mobster tried to kill her."

"I need those names, Fred." He opened a notepad on his phone. "Type them here and I'll check them out."

Fred tapped his pockets. "I don't seem to have my bifocals."

"Use these." Bryce found his glasses in front of the television. "Squint if they don't work. I need to talk to Kylie."

Fred covered her hand with his own. "I will admit that it's been a challenge keeping you out of the public spotlight, sugar. 'Fraid that's out of our hands now. You should know that your friends decided way back that we'd stand shoulder to shoulder with you if something happened. You're not alone."

He nodded to Bryce to take a chair while he pushed back from the table. He scooped up the cell and glasses and went to stand by the front window.

"I can't believe this." Kylie shook her head, looking as shocked as he felt.

Bryce spun the dining chair and straddled it,

leaning on the back but close enough to lower his voice so only Kylie could hear him.

"I think he's sincere. That creates a big problem for us." He waited until she looked up with a question in her eyes. "A while ago you didn't want to call for help because you were afraid of what would happen to trained officers. What do you think is going to happen if your friends stand shoulder to shoulder?"

"A lot of innocent people are going to get hurt."

"Yeah. I'm not saying that Fred isn't right. He is. I don't have a warrant. Compelling you to testify is something I can't do…yet. But for their sakes I think it's time you told me what you know about Xander Tenoreno that makes him so determined to kill you."

"Bryce, I really don't know anything about his business." She threaded her fingers through her blond hair. "Please believe me."

"I've read the reports of the night you were shot. Didn't you wonder why he wanted to meet in that part of Austin?" He knew the answer, but wanted to hear her personal account, too. "Maybe you'll remember something different this time."

"I went for my cat. Xander is a cruel man…at least he was five years ago when I knew him. I told the police, I never suspected that he would try to kill me. When his alibi checked out, along with all of his closest men, there was nothing anyone could do."

"What about the day-to-day operations of the Tenoreno family?" He noticed that Fred was standing at the window, arms crossed, frowning and definitely listening.

Hard of hearing old man? He doubted it.

"I lived there for a couple of months. I was on photo shoots back then. Or going to movie premieres in LA. Xander went with me everywhere, even to Fashion Week in New York. He seemed to get a high from draping himself all over me. I liked the attention at first." She rested her head on her hands, hiding her eyes from him.

"But?"

She jerked straight, throwing her head back and pushing her hair away from her face. "Do we really have to do this now? I'm a little exhausted. Actually, I'm more than exhausted and need some sleep." She pushed the chair back, grabbing her shoulder bag and standing. "You have a bed, right? I'm using it."

"Kylie—"

"I'll take that cup of coffee now." Fred jumped between him and the woman running down the hall. "She'll be better in the morning. This is a lot to process right now."

Fred's hand was plastered against Bryce's chest. Not necessarily pushing, but if he pressed forward, he'd have to knock the older man to the side.

"You need to back off." Bryce pushed the

words through a jaw clamped so tight his teeth wouldn't move.

Fred threw his hands up in surrender, gesturing toward the kitchen. "Want a cup?"

"Let me explain something. You're a guest here. Only here because of your previous service and because I can use an extra set of eyes keeping her safe. We'll reassess the situation when my partner arrives."

"Sure thing. I'll get that coffee." Fred stepped aside toward the kitchen.

Bryce followed Kylie toward the bedroom— there was only one furnished. The door was open and she was lying across the covers, arm covering her eyes. There were still a lot of lights flashing outside even with the blinds drawn shut.

"I need to move you to the middle bedroom. It's smaller, but easier to defend."

"Okay. Do you have a cot or something? I didn't see another bed."

"I'll put this mattress on the floor."

"That isn't necessary."

"Of course it is, Kylie. Don't worry about it."

She picked up the pillows and he lifted the mattress, bedding and all onto its side. She stepped out of the way and he pushed it down the hall to the smaller room.

"Keep the lights off. If someone's watching the house we might fool them as to which room you're in."

She sat on the mattress and leaned against the inside wall, pulling the sheet up to her chin. "I could really use a good soak, but I assume that's out of the question."

He nodded.

"And I don't suppose I'll be left alone?"

He shook his head. "I'll stay right here."

"All right." She plumped the pillows and twisted awkwardly to put her head down. "Is there something else, Bryce?"

"I need to see what you have inside the bag."

"Take it. There's nothing inside. You know all my secrets already." She covered her head with the covers.

He picked up the green bag, slid his back down the wall to the floor and reached for his phone, remembering Fred still had it. A couple of four-letter words went through his mind at the thought of getting back up. Then the smell of coffee got stronger. Fred sauntered his long frame down the hall.

"You know there are chairs in the other room a lot more comfortable than that floor." He handed over one cup and slurped at the other.

"I'm good. Thanks for this."

"Here's your phone and glasses. I'll be right back. My bones are too old to sit without support."

Bryce placed his frames on his face and gawked into the black brew like an old gypsy telling futures with tea leaves. He wanted a plan. Some-

thing solid. Or a reason for Tenoreno to have made a move on Kylie today.

"Why now?" he whispered as the legs of a dining chair scraped the floor. "He couldn't have known she was here. Not that fast. I just made the confirmation today."

"And by confirmation you mean?" Fred sat in the chair at the end of the hall.

"I told Kylie that she was in danger."

"How did you find her? Can I ask that?" Fred tipped the chair to two feet balancing against the wall.

"Yeah, can we both ask that?" Kylie's voice from the bedroom didn't sound interested in sleeping.

Three years of my spare time. "Facial recognition from a picture that appeared with an internet magazine feature. It was about the teen and senior program you volunteer with."

"Runs and created." Fred slurped loudly. "Does a damn fine job."

"The article said it was a community effort. It's impressive, I like what I experienced today. I take it you've been keeping Kylie behind the camera instead of in front of it?"

"I volunteered. I thought I'd convinced everyone it was more about them than me. I can't believe everyone knew."

"Everyone didn't. You've got the two other names besides myself. One's the owner of the Kof-

fee Cup and the other is the woman who runs the Billy the Kid Museum. They were watching the morning news together when I brought a disheveled young woman who didn't weigh as much as a toothpick into the shop. Praise be that those two old women don't gossip."

"Why didn't you turn me over to the police, Fred?"

"It wasn't like you'd broken any law by walking away from everything." He shrugged. "We all thought you'd been through enough. If you needed some peace and quiet, why shouldn't it be here where we could watch out for you?"

"I can't ever tell you how much these years have meant to me. They changed my life."

Bryce could hear the emotional catch in her tone. Kylie was about to cry. He did admire what the people of Hico had done, and everything that she'd done to make her life meaningful. It was much better than the fast lane she'd been in as a teen model.

None of it mattered.

Kylie's location had been discovered and it wasn't because of him. He hadn't had much time to think things through since the firefight. But now that he could...he'd called only the major to inform him. *He* hadn't informed anyone else. The one call he'd received at Kylie's that morning was from the Austin PD telling him they'd lost Tenoreno.

"Fred, have y'all noticed anyone new in town? Any strangers here longer than they should be?"

"You mean besides you? Nope."

"This doesn't make sense."

"What doesn't?" Kylie asked.

"How did they find you? Not only that. How did they find you *today*? It's illogical." Bryce's brain was at home with computers and patterns and logic.

"Did you do anything different today, girlie? Besides trying to lose this fellow across the fields?"

Bryce heard the sheets rustle behind him, then Kylie was at the opposite side of the doorway. Hair tussled as if she'd just awakened and had tossed and turned all night. The house wasn't an icebox. It was more like an old unit that barely put out cold air, yet she still wore her long sleeves and covered up.

"Nothing different. I mowed the lawn, started trimming a couple of dead limbs, talked to Bryce." She finger-combed her hair while she explained, smoothing it back into place. "When he left me alone, I came up with the idea of walking away. I've had plans in place for years. But with him watching the place like a stalker, I had to improvise."

"Looks like the only thing different in this equation is you, son."

They both looked at him. Eyebrows raised. Eyes

opened wide. Expecting something that resembled an answer. It wasn't against the rules for him to share what he knew. And they knew most of it anyway.

"The Austin PD has been tailing Tenoreno since Thomas Rosco's death. He shook the car following him today. I told you that this morning," he said to Kylie.

"You're right, though. It's a bit coincidental that someone tries to kill Kylie after all these years. And on the very day you show your hand." Fred smirked.

"Here's the other thing that's bothering me. Why so public?"

"That was an awful lot of firepower for something that could have been handled with a single blade as a home invasion. No offense, Kylie." Fred set his empty coffee mug on the floor and brought all his chair legs back to earth.

Bryce hadn't touched his own coffee. It was cool enough now to just gulp it for the caffeine. Which he did.

"Why would they want the entire town to know I'd been killed?"

"Exactly." He had to ponder the question awhile.

In fact, every question they asked just led to more questions and no answers.

Bryce unfolded his glasses, put them in place and then checked his phone. No messages from

Jesse or Major Parker. He'd missed his Saturday afternoon call with his mom and dad. That was it. He sent the names Fred had typed into his message to headquarters in Austin. Same thing with the car licenses from the hotels.

Ironically, if he hadn't been on this assignment, he'd be the one sitting in Waco. He'd be utilizing the information available for the Rangers and collecting data. He'd find out if any of these Hico citizens had a connection to Xander or Paul Tenoreno.

Fred was on his phone. When he noticed Bryce looking at him he said, "Calling my daughter. She might actually be a little worried." He put the phone to his ear and walked toward the back of the house.

"Where's your cell?"

"I don't have one. Just the landline and the laptop." Kylie adjusted her position, sitting crosslegged in the doorway. "The kids instant message me online if they want to talk. Adults call."

"I don't think I've met anyone over twelve that doesn't have a cell phone."

"Believe me. It might have been one of the hardest things to give up. After running away and starting completely over with a thousand dollars in my pocket." She crossed her arms to match her legs and rested her head on the wall. "I used to have two. Cells, that is. One was completely for social media and the press, my agent, my favor-

ite photographers, my publicist. Only my closest friends had my personal number. Even that had to be changed every three or four months when a weird fan would call or post it to the world."

"Do you miss it or ever want to go back?"

"I can't go back if I did want to. My skin is definitely…flawed."

He searched her perfect skin. No freckles, no acne, no discolorations. He reached out to tap the tiny crinkles around her eyes. "Flawed?"

"You're funny. Didn't you say you'd seen my file? Doesn't it have pictures of the gunshots?"

"Oh, yeah. Couldn't you still model, though?"

"I don't want to go back. That life was never real. It belonged to Sissy Jorgenson, my stage name and persona. It turned everyone I ever loved into money-starved…" She had been looking around the room, sort of staring at nothing. Then she locked eyes with his. "I couldn't see what it did to me while I was living it. I was willing to marry Xander because he didn't need anything from me. At least that's what I thought. I was just a dumb kid."

He shook his head, agreeing, letting her assume he knew what she had gone through. But he didn't.

"I have a scar," he threw out.

"You might have some from that burn you got today," she teased.

"It's not much, but it's never gone away." He pulled up his jeans leg and slid off his boot, push-

ing down his sock. "When I was a kid a rattler got me. See it? Those two white spots."

"No appendicitis? No shotgun blast to your back?"

"Shotgun? Why would you think—"

"From all those husbands and boyfriends chasing you out windows, silly."

Again with the teasing. He was glad she could laugh. Her life had been turned upside down five years ago. If it had happened to him and then began repeating itself, he didn't know how he would have handled it.

"It's just stuff, you know. Everything over there can be replaced."

"Except the Cadillac," Fred said from the corner. "She's a beaut. Am I right? Did you see her?"

"Except the Cadillac," Bryce repeated. "That's our answer. It was the car."

Chapter Nine

Kylie tried to sleep. Her body told her she should. She was exhausted from the day's activities and mentally tired of playing the games she'd run away from so long ago. She was also tired of everyone trying to manipulate her. Even Fred while trying to protect her. If she walked away from the people who had stood by her all these years...

Was she betraying them?

Or protecting them as Bryce had pointed out?

Now sleep was impossible because a total stranger was pacing the halls, tapping on his cell, cursing at whoever he was texting to answer back. Jesse Ryder was Bryce's partner. And yet, he'd walked through the door and Bryce had barreled past him, Fred not far behind.

"They're checking something out on the Cadillac." She tried getting his attention from her protected space. Bryce had reminded her to stay put with a graphic description of what the gun had

done to her house. So she was close to the hallway door with her back against the closet. Remembering the hole in the wall made her want to sleep inside the bathtub.

"Where?" Jesse stopped as he walked past the door. "What Cadillac?"

"My house. Across the street and two doors down. There's a flowerpot of marigolds on the front porch—well, there used to be. Come to think about it, I think someone knocked them off. The porch light is on."

"Every porch light is on after what happened earlier." He typed more on his cell. "You shouldn't have made it out of that attack alive. Or was Johnson exaggerating?"

"No, I think he got the details right. The headline will probably read something like Giant Hole in the Wall, Refrigerator Saves Couple. I think there are pictures now."

The new guy barely cracked a smile. He looked like he was in an old spaghetti western, one boot propped against the wall, head down rolling a ciggy. Only instead of a cigarette, he was focused on a cell phone.

"At least you're not trending yet. But you're right. There are definitely pictures." Ever vigilant of his surroundings, he stood straight at the slightest sound. His hand would go to his holster on his hip, then he'd relax against the wall again.

"I heard you tried to walk cross-country to get away from him."

"It was the only thing I could think of at the time."

"I can think of a much easier solution...just come back with us. Do you know *why* they had to look at this car?" Jesse asked.

"It's stolen. I know that much."

"You said it was your house. Did you steal it?" He left her to walk to the front room again.

"The official story is that I borrowed it." She spoke a little louder so he could hear her around the corner.

He nodded his head. He wasn't as tall as Bryce, not quite as built through the shoulders. She drew her knees to her chest, trying to stretch her back and get comfortable. It didn't feel right lying on the mattress with the new guy watching. Even if she had all her clothes on, including her shoes.

"I have a question." She waited for him to nod that he'd answer. "Do they really teach how to calculate walking speeds or something like that in Ranger school?"

His confused expression was all she needed to know that Bryce had been full of it earlier. She silently laughed at herself for halfway believing him.

"So what's so important about the car? I'm guessing that you didn't steal it today."

"Five years ago."

"That's when you— Is it Tenoreno's?"

She nodded. "I told Bryce about it just before they attacked. He had some revelation about fifteen minutes before you got here. Fred argued with him that it wasn't possible. Don't ask me what it is, because they wouldn't tell me. Bryce said he wanted to confirm his suspicions."

"I guess we both wait then." Phone in his pocket, he began his patrol again.

Resting her head and eyes, she could hear his boots walk up and down the hall, pause at the front window, circle through the kitchen and repeat. Silently, she debated the pros and cons of going to Waco with Bryce.

No matter how hurt Fred's feelings might be, leaving with Bryce was her only logical option. What if the gunmen had opened fire on the event earlier today? With that thought, she knew leaving was her only choice. They were under orders to keep an eye on her so they wouldn't let her leave alone. One way or another it had to be with them.

Drifting off, she was yanked back when Bryce and Fred burst into the house, arguing loud enough to wake the block. Well, if anyone had actually gone back to bed.

"I tell you it's not possible. That GPS locator has a short range. They wouldn't be able to pick it up in Austin." Fred yelled.

"Don't you get it? They could have followed her that first night. If it's short range, they just drive

until they find it." Bryce yelled back. "Someone's probably known where she was this entire time. It's not a coincidence that I show up and all hell breaks loose."

There was a loud piercing whistle that got the men to shut up. Kylie left the protection of the bedroom, stopping at the edge of the hall. She didn't want to draw eyes back to herself and be sent to her room like a child.

"It can't be right," Fred repeated.

"Can you explain what we're talking about?" Jesse bent the window blinds looking outside.

"It's not good. There's a GPS locater on Tenoreno's Cadillac." Bryce answered him, keeping his back to everyone.

"A tracking system? How strong? Wait. Why didn't we locate her when she stole the car and disappeared five years ago?" Jesse was at attention. Did he realize his fingers had drifted to the gun at his side?

"GPS. Either law enforcement wasn't looking or it wasn't reported stolen."

Kylie could see the tension in the way he was standing. And the way he was looking out the back windows. Did he expect to see another targeting laser pointed at the house?

"You've been driving a stolen car for five years and no one's caught on?" Jesse looked straight at her. The other two men's heads turned, too.

"Don't look at me. I don't drive the blasted

thing. It never leaves my garage. I avoid it as much as possible. The engine can't even crank." An eerie feeling was creeping up the back of her neck. There was something terribly wrong with what they were saying. Maybe she was too tired to read between the lines, but even then…

The men's reactions were beginning to scare her.

"I'm the one who charged the battery last week when you got here and made certain it would run. Just in case, you know, she needed it one day soon," Fred said.

"Like tonight?" Bryce said strongly again.

"What if—what if he didn't know about it?" she whispered and searched their faces getting their attention. "Xander hadn't had the car very long. He'd been bragging about winning it. That's why I took the convertible, because he seemed so excited about it. But he was out of the country when I left."

"By the time he got back, I'd disconnected the battery." Fred scratched his scruffy chin.

Why did it all matter, though? How they found her wasn't as important as the fact that they *had* found her. Right?

"I don't understand why this is so important. I'll come up with a new plan after the state attorneys hear my pathetic cry of 'I don't know anything' a thousand more times."

"If the locator drew someone's attention, they

found you pretty easily after it was reconnected."
Jesse was oh so matter-of-fact with his explanation. "If it didn't, someone's following Bryce."

"Someone? You mean Xander."

"Or the guy he won the car from. Either way, someone out there wants you dead. They just aren't very good at it." Jesse crossed his arms and leaned against the wall.

That can't be true.

"Dammit, Ryder." Bryce moved to her side. "She's as white as a sheet."

"He tried to kill me. I know it was Xander. It had to be." Kylie hadn't experienced a panic attack. There was no time for one, either time her life had been threatened.

Bryce looked into her eyes, forcing her to focus on him. "We should keep all the possibilities open. Do you have any idea who else would want to kill you tonight *or* five years ago?"

Right this very second her pulse raced, her breath seemed to be cut off at her nose and she could barely stand. She might really pass out. "I'm walking across the room and sitting on that couch. Don't try to stop me."

Nobody touched her. Of course, having her hands splayed in a don't-touch-me position might have warned them that she was serious.

Bryce motioned for his partner to check outside. Jesse walked out the door without a word. Fred worriedly rubbed his chin and took a seat at the

table. She could see he was blaming himself for not catching the GPS gadget earlier. His comfort would have to wait.

Right this second she had to wrap her head around an entirely new possibility. Did someone besides Xander want to kill her? Very publicly making a show of hurting the people around her. Who could want that? Do that?

An unknown person who hated her? Five years ago, Xander wanting her dead had been hard enough to live with, but at least she understood. Now she had to think about someone else managing to get close to accomplishing it…twice.

"You have to be wrong, Bryce. I didn't know anyone who hated me like my ex-husband."

BRYCE TOOK A dining chair and set it close to her, straddling it as he had earlier, arms folded over its back. He dropped his right hand to cover one of hers that was resting on the couch.

"I know I'm right. Sure, there are a lot of possibilities. Just trust me. We can't argue any longer." He lowered his voice so Fred wouldn't interrupt him. "I need to get you under the state's protection before there's another incident."

"But—"

"I get it, Kylie. I do. But for your protection and for everybody around you, come with me. Make your deal, talk with the attorneys, have them guarantee it in writing. Then let them decide what

you know or don't. It's the only way I can keep you safe."

She nodded.

"He's right," Fred said from the dinette. "I wish there was something I could do."

Bryce stood, offering his hand to help Kylie up. "Get your bag. We're leaving now." He turned to Fred. "There is something you can do. We'll be working with Hico on the crime scene." He removed the Cadillac ignition key from the key ring. "Before anyone gets here, disconnect the GPS tracker and move the car to a safe place. Somewhere no one will get hurt if someone comes looking."

"I know the perfect place."

"Good. Keep it to yourself for now." He clapped the man on the shoulder.

Fred did the same. "We're trusting you with our girl."

"Yes, sir. You have my word."

"I'm ready." Kylie gave Fred a hug. "Stay safe, my friend."

"You betcha. Don't worry 'bout a thing. We'll all still be here when you come home. And I'll get that hole patched just as soon as the cops are done with the place."

Bryce waited at the door during the embrace. Kylie joined him, putting her hand on his shoulder just like they'd done at her house. Hard to believe it had just been a few hours earlier.

"We don't know if they're still out there. If I stop this time, get as close to my body as you can. Become my second skin. Got it?"

"Yeah, I'm good."

"Straight to Jesse's truck."

Through the door, Jesse was at his elbow. He unlocked the doors, taking his place in the driver's seat. When Bryce joined Kylie in the backseat she seemed a little surprised, but scooted over to the other side.

"Keep your heads down, you two. If we're lucky, we're out of town with no incident."

Bryce slumped in the seat, and gestured for Kylie to stretch out across it. There wasn't any hesitation as she leaned on his chest and let him support her on the trip out of town.

Once they passed the east city limit sign, Bryce put away his weapon and tried to relax for their passenger's sake. Kylie sat on her side, but watched the town disappear behind them.

"Don't forget to buckle up, kiddies," Jesse taunted. "Sun's coming up. Going to be a beautiful day."

"Maybe for you," Kylie mumbled.

"Anybody following?" Bryce looked over his shoulder, too. He couldn't distinguish any vehicles that might not be using their headlights.

"Nada. Maybe they weren't watching the house?"

He met Jesse's glance in the mirror. His part-

ner had said that for Kylie's peace of mind but didn't believe it any more than Bryce. Someone was watching her house. They'd been waiting for Kylie to return, so they knew Bryce was with her. So logic followed that they knew where Bryce lived.

"You can grab a nap if you want." Bryce squeezed her hand.

She smiled but her eyes were full of sadness.

"You'll be back, Kylie. I promise."

Jesse frowned and shook his head. Kylie turned in the big seat of the extended cab and withdrew. The hour drive seemed to take as long as all of the previous day.

Uncertainty reared its ugly head. Had he done the professional thing? The right thing? He wouldn't be able to answer that until this situation was resolved. But he was certain about one small piece…he'd done the best thing for Kylie.

Her life was in danger and his gut told him these people weren't about to stop now that they had her in their sights.

Chapter Ten

Austin, three days later

The location was supposed to be secret. Who leaked it didn't matter. On the way inside the first day, Kylie and her attorney had been swamped by the press. She was the story of the hour. The headlines screamed her name—or Sissy's name.

At night in her hotel room, she alternated between glued to the television scanning the news for a mention of her name and handing the remote to the guard posted outside her room. The men guarding her rotated through the night and got a laugh at passing the baton—remote—to each other. All of them were gentlemen.

None of them was Bryce.

Missing her friends in Hico was natural. She'd known and worked with them for a long time. But Bryce? Why should she miss him? He'd told her to trust him and that he'd have a plan in place soon.

Then promptly agreed to hand her off to become someone else's problem.

Okay, that was harsh. He hadn't really agreed. She'd heard him arguing with his commander who'd said the men in Company F had been making it a habit of getting too close to their assignments. Whatever that meant. In the end, she'd been given a few clothes, a hamburger and escorted to headquarters in Austin after a phone call to her lawyer.

No phone calls since she'd been here. Not even a phone in her room.

It didn't matter how illogical it was, she had been attracted to Bryce since she'd first met him. And since she'd first admired him mowing that dust bowl of a lawn Mrs. Mackey owned.

Oh well. It wasn't to be. Whatever happened now, she doubted she'd see the tall law enforcement officer again.

Day two in Austin wasn't any better. Everyone wanted to know where she'd been or why she'd been hiding. Did she fear for her life? Were the men guarding her or was she under arrest? She had ignored shouts from the press before. Ignored the many photographs of her taken each time she'd been in public.

It was harder this time. Harder to ignore all the questions because they weren't obnoxious or too personal. Each of them was pertinent.

But she couldn't answer them…she didn't know the answers.

In fact, she had more questions today than ever before.

They walked through the front door with her escort—the one that did not include either of the men who had found or rescued her. Their meeting was on the sixth floor and they took the elevator. Two rangers—she hadn't caught their names—crowded the front and refused to allow anyone else to board. She stood next to her lawyer, who had dropped everything to help her the past three days.

Everyone was silent. There wasn't even silly elevator music to help pass the time. Kylie was nervous, but next to her friend and lawyer, she looked like the calm and collected one. Her guards dropped them off at the door and another officer showed them to a conference room.

Lizbeth Reynolds opened her briefcase, took out a yellow notepad and her pen. She straightened them a couple of times after setting the briefcase on the floor. No one else had arrived yet. She poured a glass of water from one of four pitchers on the long oval table.

"Want some?"

"No thanks. I had three cups of coffee watching the news at my motel."

"I saw some of the highlights. You look good and have the sympathy of the people."

Sympathy of the people?

"Oh, Lizbeth. If it was you who told the press that I was back in town, don't ever tell me. You were such a good friend to me. You'll never know how much I appreciate you taking my case on such short notice."

"Don't ever think of me as a friend in the past tense again. I'm not certain why you want me. You'd be much better off with a criminal defense attorney."

Lizbeth patted her hand, but didn't deny being the one to leak the location. It was okay. Especially since she was right. The press and population were on her side. It would be harder for the state to compel her to do anything. And if she had to, she'd meet with the reporters and share part of her story.

Of course, it would also be harder for her to disappear again. One step at a time. She had to power through this particular mess first.

The court reporter took her seat. The attorneys filed through the door. Kylie could feel Lizbeth's legs shaking. The men kept standing while the judge entered.

Everyone was introduced for the record, then the judge said they were going to recess for five minutes, excusing the court reporter from the room. He waved everyone to sit. Confusion followed by an immediate burst of fright hitting her like a tsunami.

"Let's keep this as informal as possible," the judge said. "If things get out of hand, I'll call Joyce back in here and we'll start from the beginning."

Kylie looked at Lizbeth who drew a question mark on her pad, shrugged and shook her head with no explanation. Kylie sat on her hands not wanting to appear nervous. But she was.

"Truth of the matter, gentlemen," the judge continued, "is that you have no case. Miss Scott has continued to tell you that she knows nothing of her ex-husband's business dealings. She told all those involved five years ago and she's continuing to do so now."

"Your Honor—"

"Yeah, I'm not finished." He shook his head. "In fact, I'm utterly ashamed that you've yanked this young woman away from her quiet life in Hico." He turned and looked at Kylie. "Nice little town, some of the best pie in Texas. My wife and I drive through there to visit our son."

"I'll tell Allison you mentioned it."

"Nice. Real nice." He took off his glasses tossing them to the table. They scooted past the second lawyer who stuck his hand out and caught them. "You see, fellows, you're trying to tell me that you'll drop the charges of auto theft if Miss Scott testifies. This is where your brief lost me. Not only did you *not* find the 1964 Cadillac convertible on Miss Scott's property, you lack a vehicle theft report. The owner claims the car is still on one of his properties."

Kylie's leg was being gripped so hard by Lizbeth she'd be black-and-blue the next day. Then her attorney excitedly smiled and tapped her pen on the yellow pad so fast, Kylie was afraid it would fly and hit the judge in the eye.

"I know you're excited, Miss Reynolds, but again, I'm not finished." He turned to The Three Stooges of attorneys. "I'm advising you to withdraw your request. Now. Once I bring Joyce back in here…well, you don't want to know what I'm going to say."

He motioned that it was someone else's turn to speak.

"If Your Honor would issue the search warrant—"

"There won't be a search warrant for Mr. Tenoreno's property. He has several, including in other countries. Without the car or a theft report…"

"Then Your Honor leaves us no choice but to withdraw all protection from Miss Scott."

"Good. You on the end, call Joyce back inside, please."

The reporter took her position. The charges were officially dismissed. The lawyers put away their papers. Lizbeth was shaking with excitement. And Kylie was utterly stunned.

"Everybody can go," the judge announced. The

group stood and the judge tapped Kylie's arm. "Mind staying a minute, Miss Scott?"

"Not at all, should Lizbeth…?"

"No, it's nothing official. I just want to apologize for these jackasses."

"That's not necessary. Really. Everything's fine." She turned to Lizbeth, wanting to leave.

"I'll wait for you downstairs in the lobby." Lizbeth smiled and waved.

"Why don't we go into the office?" He held the door for her.

"I can't believe what just happened. It was all so fast my head is still spin—"

She preceded the judge through the entryway. He gave her a little shove and backed out, quickly closing the door. The term spinning was no longer figurative. She literally spun to the side and into Xander's arms. She pushed and shoved attempting a release, but his grip got tighter and more hurtful.

When she stopped fighting him, he released her.

The aikido that she'd studied had disappeared. None of the auto-defense moves that she'd practiced had kicked in. She sought a level of calm by smoothing her dress and pretending not to pay attention. Just under the surface of her movements she was aware of her ex's every turn.

Her nerves were jumpier than a magic jumping bean she'd had once as a little girl.

"Dear God, what have you done to yourself?" he spat meanly. "You've gotten fat."

She could handle his harsh words. She'd heard them before, even when she was much under a normal weight and all her bones stuck out. She could take anything he served.

"I see you still employ that wimpy lawyer who lost you everything in the divorce."

"Lizbeth is my friend, and we both know what happened in the divorce. She had nothing to do with it. Why are you here, Xander?"

"It's simple. I want an annulment. We were never married in the church, but that doesn't matter to the church."

"Sure. Do you have the papers with you? Or you can send them to Lizbeth's office and she'll know how to find me. You didn't have to go through these scare tactics to get your way. I'm not that same inexperienced child bride that you married."

"You aren't, are you? But I'm only interested in the annulment."

"Can I go now?"

"I want it done today." He paused, which was unlike him. "The papers are at the house. I, um… so you took the Cadillac?"

"That boat has sailed, partner. No proof. The judge threw out the case." She calculated how long it would take to reach the door.

Which door? The one behind him that she knew

led to the conference room or the two on her right? *What if one is a closet?* Would he catch her? *Yes.*

"Unless he has a theft report." He took out a folded piece of paper from his shirt pocket. "Which I just happen to have."

"I don't know where your car is and I don't care." She inched a little closer to the door with a light under it. "I left it at my house and when the police arrived, it had been stolen. How's that for irony for you?"

He crossed the short distance between them and raised his hand. She'd been on the receiving end of that slap once or twice. It wouldn't happen again. She moved at the last minute and Xander's fist hit the wall.

"Tell me where the Cadillac is." He steadily raised his voice, talking through gritted teeth. "Dammit. I want...my car."

"Then *find* your car. But leave me alone. Send your church papers to my lawyer. You're done in my life. Do you hear me? We're done. You can't hurt me anymore."

Defiant words for the abundance of fright fluttering inside her. Back to the wall, she scooted sideways until her hand felt the door handle.

"You're forgetting that I can do anything I want." He supported his hand, vigorously massaging the knuckles. "Nobody will stop me."

Never taking her eyes off him, she slipped through, closing the door behind her. She wanted to collapse in a ball right there in the hallway. But she had to get away from him. She ran, heels echoing through the empty halls until she found the restroom.

Inside she got into the last stall and slid the bolt. It wouldn't protect her. She knew it, but had to have something between her and Xander. She leaned against the wall and cried.

All because of fear. She hated fear and the way it ate at every level of confidence a person could muster.

The rest of the afternoon was a blur. She might have stayed where she was if Lizbeth hadn't eventually found her. Frantic herself, they held on to each other and got someone who worked in the building to call a cab and let them out the back.

The rangers were gone.

That meant no protection.

Bryce was wrong. He couldn't keep his word and Xander wanted her dead more than he wanted that stupid Cadillac.

Chapter Eleven

Waco

Being called to the head of Company F's office had never felt like a visit to the principal before. The difference this time was that he'd broken some basic rules, not orders. Rules put in place to protect witnesses and officers.

"You're playing with fire, Bryce."

"Sir?"

Major Parker put both palms on his desk and pushed himself to stand, staring Bryce in the eye and not blinking. Bryce was about to be reprimanded, an action he wasn't used to but was determined to accept. Even if he wasn't volunteering information about what he'd done. Or apologizing.

"You know I've been calling in favors to get you back on this case. I understand what it's like to give your word to someone. I explained that the state's attorneys felt it best to remove you from Kylie Scott's protection detail."

"Because she trusted me too much? That makes no sense—"

Parker's stare made it unpleasant enough that Bryce shut up without finishing. How the man stood taller was one of those mystical practices no one wanted to experience. The air got sucked out of the room somehow and Bryce felt ten years old again.

Parker put his hands behind his back and met Bryce boot toe to boot toe. "Did I give you the impression you could speak yet, Lieutenant?"

A question that if answered meant he was in the dog house. Yet by not answering did he look like he didn't understand? Or maybe he did, but Bryce chose to stand at attention, eyes forward not meeting the major's.

"Hacking into the state's records to find out where your girlfriend—"

"Miss Scott."

"—is being held is against every protocol we have in place. You've been suspended for two weeks."

"Suspended, sir? But this is my first infraction."

"And it's a severe one, Bryce."

"But she's not being held anywhere at all, sir. They let her go. Didn't even bother to give her a ride back to Hico this morning."

"I know." The major put his hands on his hips,

seeming less stern than seconds before. "We have orders to stay clear of the situation."

Realization hit him over the head. Severe discipline allowed Bryce to keep his word. He could help Kylie without officially involving the Rangers. Two weeks without pay was definitely going to make a dent in his budget, but helping her was worth it.

"Thank you, sir. I guess vacation wouldn't do?" His commander's stern look made him follow up with, "I get it. I completely understand, sir."

"Since our computer expert will be out of the office for two weeks, I'm going to remind you that your access to our database will remain active. You should refrain from using that access." He paused. "At least as much as possible. And then there's the matter of your badge. I think you should have Vivian secure it for you. Damn, I think she's at lunch." He looked toward the empty desk of the Company's secretary. "Just bring it by tomorrow. You understand what I'm saying, Bryce?"

"Yes, sir."

Major Josh Parker sat behind his desk and picked up a plain number two pencil. He threaded it through his fingers and began his habitual twirling. Bryce didn't think he'd been dismissed. The normal sign that the major was finished was when his feet went to the corner of his desk. The Company called it his thinking mode.

"I gave her my word, too. I'm counting on you to keep it. But if you get into trouble…" The pencil cracked over his knuckles. "I have vacation time."

"Got it. Thank you, sir." Bryce was grateful, but not surprised that his commanding officer was willing to break the rules to help keep his word. That's the kind of man he was. One of the true good guys.

"Turn the files you're working on over to Vivian. One last thing." He stood, palms flat on his desk, the apparent fury of a man who meant what he said behind every word. "There won't be a next time. I don't need men who go behind my back and disobey orders."

"No, sir. It won't happen again."

"Just bring the problem to me, Bryce." He sat again and crossed his ankles on the corner of the old wooden desk. "I usually know what I'm doing."

"Thank you, Major."

Bryce took care of the case files and explained the situation to Jesse. His partner cursed that he'd be working alone and then said he was due vacation time. Bryce spent fifteen minutes convincing him he'd call if he got into a tough spot.

As soon as he was out of the building he called Fred. "Did Kylie contact you?"

"Yeah. Said she was catching a bus to Dallas. Said it was too dangerous for her to come home."

"Dammit, why didn't she call me? I could have picked her up, taken care of things."

"I think that's why she asked me *not* to call you. Repeated the part about being dangerous for everybody and that it was better for her to start over." Fred paused but Bryce knew what was coming. "Alone."

"What bus line and what time did the bus leave?"

"She called right before boarding the nonstop. Should be passing through Waco in about half an hour. I can get to Dallas and drag her back here. Damn, I wish that girl had a cell phone. Would be handy about now."

"I'll take care of it. You said you had her place cleaned up?"

"Everything's set back to rights." Fred's voice perked up. "Everybody pitched in."

"There's one more thing I need you to do. If we're going to catch the person who's after Kylie, it's going to take a lot of cooperation." Bryce got into his truck, the hands-free connected and he headed out of the parking lot.

"I don't think you'll have a problem finding it."

"Yeah, but how do people feel about moving out of their houses for a couple of days?" It was a drastic plan, but he didn't think he had a chance getting Kylie to go along with it if anyone was in danger. And to prevent someone getting hurt... they simply couldn't be around.

"You mean evacuate the block?"

"As much as possible. And we need a system where people around town check in."

"You mean a phone tree? I think the Methodist church and the schools have one for bad weather. I'll get Allison to work on that. What do you think these men are going to do, hold the town hostage?"

"Whatever's necessary. I'm putting a great deal off on you, Fred. I know I'm asking a lot."

"She's a good woman. She deserves to be free of this. You take care of her."

"I will. Don't look for us until tomorrow."

"We'll be ready."

The hands-free disconnected about the time Bryce pulled in front of the mobile phone store. He added a line to his bill and got the phone activated, charging it in the truck. It took longer than he'd anticipated.

The entire time he stood there answering questions he thought about Kylie. If he couldn't find her…

What would he do? What *could* he do?

He had no claim on her. He wanted to help, but if she refused could he catch the person who wanted to harm her? After all the publicity she'd received in the past three days, he doubted she could easily disappear. Then again, she'd done it once just by running out of gas.

Flipping his lights and siren on, he tore past Baylor University and used the on-ramp for I-35. Flying down the highway, he kept his eyes open for her bus. It had to have passed through the city by then. Just past the Lacy Lakeview exit, he got behind a bus and it eased to the side of the road.

The driver met him on the shoulder holding paperwork. Bryce displayed his badge and waved that things were okay. "We're good. Mind if I take a look at your passengers?"

"Whatever floats your boat." The driver tucked his folder under his arm and lit a cigarette, taking advantage of the break.

Bryce climbed the steps, excited that he was about to see Kylie again. Just how much he wanted to see her surprised him, but not as much as looking at all the faces and being disappointed she wasn't among them. He didn't have a picture of her to show and ask the passengers if they'd seen her at the bus station.

"You'll be back underway momentarily, folks. We're looking for a woman, blonde, twenty-six years old, about my height. You might have seen her in the news recently."

He took his time looking everybody over, wondering if she'd used a disguise or had maybe dyed her hair. That's when he saw a man's finger clandestinely pointing across the aisle. Bryce walked as quietly as possible across the rubber floorboards. Whoever was there—Kylie or a criminal—they didn't want him to know they were on the bus.

"What did the woman do?" someone asked behind him.

He was even with the row and recognized Kylie even with her head between her knees. "She didn't trust the right man."

She popped up when she heard his voice. "You can't force me to leave with you. I've done absolutely nothing wrong. A judge already said that and mentioned that further interference in my life might be considered harassment."

"You're right. If you don't come with me by your own free will, you'll just run away again."

"Oh, give him another chance, honey," an older woman three rows in front of her said. "He looks like he means it."

"Don't go if he hit you. They never stop. No matter what they say," a woman who needed to wash stated flatly.

"It's nothing like that," Kylie tried to explain. "We're not a couple. He's a Texas Ranger."

"Snatch him up, girl. Those guys have job security," the older woman said.

"What do you say, Kylie? Let's talk. If you don't want to stay, I'll drive you to Dallas."

"You can't beat that offer," someone in the crowd said.

"Whatever you want, lady, but I gotta get this bus movin' again," the driver said from up front.

"Come on, Kylie." He held out his hand and smiled.

She placed her fingers in his palm and scooted to the aisle. Her blue bag was hooked over her shoulder. She had a death grip on the overnight bag they'd purchased the day she'd left Hico.

"I'll talk. That's all I'm promising."

The bus clapped.

"It's like a fairy tale."

"Or that movie, you remember...he comes in and whooshes her away."

"That's not romantic."

"We're really not a couple—" Kylie tried. "I barely know him."

One of the younger passengers stuck their phone in the air obviously recording them. He faced the young woman and pulled Kylie to a stop.

"Actually, she took one look at me with my shirt off and couldn't keep her hands off me."

"You were sunburned." She looked at everyone but him. "I rubbed lotion on— What are you doing?"

He put one hand around her waist and the other gently at her throat, then whispered, "Roll with me, Kylie. It's all part of the plan."

"Wha—"

His lips captured whatever she intended to say.

There were ooohs and ahhs all around them, he heard more clapping, felt the bus rock a little with the foot stomping. But what he felt…

The softest lips he'd ever kissed were right… there. He didn't want to break free of them. She parted her lips slightly and he took advantage. He teased her tongue into dancing with him, holding back because of where they were. His hand slid to the back of her neck. His fingers spread through her silky hair.

There might have been more, but a firm grip on his shoulder pulled him away.

"Take it outside, pal," the driver said. "You sure you want to go with this guy, Miss?"

Kylie nodded, turned and squeezed by him to get off the bus.

The young woman recording it all dropped the phone in her lap.

"How fast can you post that for me?"

"Couple of minutes," she answered, already typing.

"Would you tag me? Bryce T. Johnson, Waco."

"Sure. Want me to tag your lady?"

It's all part of the plan.

"Great idea. She used to be a model but lives in Hico now. Sissy Jorgenson."

Yep, all part of the plan.

Chapter Twelve

"What the hell was that all about?" Kylie didn't know if she was upset because of the kiss or because the passengers on the bus were tapping on the windows and taking her picture.

Bryce pulled her farther off the road as the bus left.

"Seriously, Bryce. Why did you do that? Why were they taking my picture?"

"It's part of my plan."

"Then kissing me makes perfect sense." *Of course it didn't.* "I thought we were going to talk about your *possible* plan? Talk about it, not just start perfecting it."

"I'll be honest—"

"Oh please, let's."

"—perfecting is real nice." He winked at her. "I've already put the plan in motion. The first part was to let your enemy know where you were and social media took care of that."

"And the first step was making a public statement that I'm heading to Dallas. So whatever plan I had when I arrived isn't any good."

"Did you have a plan once you got there?"

He still hadn't put the truck in gear. They sat on the shoulder with cars and trucks zooming by. It wasn't the safest place in the world, especially to have a discussion or argument. His question was another that she didn't have an answer to. A bus ride to Dallas was cheap, saved money, got her out of Austin and more than anything else gave her time to think.

Shoot. In the two hours on the bus she'd only thought about one person... Bryce. She wasn't even that upset about being ambushed by Xander the day before. She'd slept soundly for the first time since this mess began.

Why? She should have been scared after his threats. But she wasn't when she thought of this man who had come to stop her from running away. He'd raced after a bus because he had a plan. He'd kissed her because he had a plan.

"Maybe we should talk over coffee or maybe something to eat?"

"I can handle that. I'll even buy." He put the truck in gear, left the flashing lights on and passed cars as they slowed on the right.

"I'm not starving, Bryce."

"Hell...I am. Now you got me hungry for

Bush's fried chicken. It's a staple here in Waco. Ever had it?"

She shook her head. His certainty about what to do seemed to be wearing off. He fidgeted a little, not much, but enough to make her aware of it.

"Look, I…um…I want to say I'm sorry for not sticking with you to Austin. The guys from headquarters took good care of you, though. Right? I tried to find someone who was on your detail, but I wasn't quick enough. They rotated them with short hours."

"I noticed. They didn't allow me a phone in the room and barely time alone with my lawyer. It's okay. I'm fine." Should she tell him about Xander?

Maybe not while he was still behind the wheel. He wasn't really speeding and when traffic thinned down, he cut his flashing lights off. His chicken place wasn't far off the highway and when he rolled his window down the smell made her glad he'd sped most of the way.

"You're heading through the drive-through? Are we going to talk in the truck?"

"I thought I'd take you to my place. We can hold a conversation and avoid people taking your picture."

"I notice the cut from my house is healing." He didn't have it covered with a bandage any longer. "Are we close to your apartment?"

"We're right around the corner." Bryce ordered

enough for a small army, including a gallon of iced tea.

He exaggerated a bit with his claim that his house was right around the corner. Maybe that's how they measured things in Texas, but he lived a good fifteen minutes southwest of the highway. The smell of the chicken was absolutely driving her nuts.

The cul-de-sac on Hidden Oaks Circle had four huge houses. At first, Kylie thought they'd made a wrong turn.

"Bryce, did you forget to tell me something?"

"Like what?"

"Are you married? All this food, this big house... Do you still live at home?"

He laughed and pushed a gate opener. "I live alone. I haven't even got a dog."

"Oh, why not? I'd get one if I could." She looked around the perfectly manicured lawn and porch. Everything seemed to have a specific place, laid out nice and neat.

"You have a great yard in Hico, why didn't you get one?" He pushed a second remote and opened the garage but didn't pull inside.

"I've always wanted a dog but I traveled too much and never had a yard. Then when I started over, I thought I'd have to leave town in a moment's notice and it wouldn't be fair to leave a dog behind."

He put the truck in Park and turned toward her.

"A lot of people wouldn't think of that. They'd just get one anyway." Did he want to kiss her again? He hooked her hair behind her ear and brushed her cheek. "And I work too much. Long hours and a lot of weekends. Let's eat."

"Can we eat outside? I've been cooped up in stuffy rooms since Sunday." She walked around the end of the house and another section of the yard opened up with a pool. "Really? That's just a little overkill for a bachelor."

"I got the house for a song and it's a great investment. I needed it for taxes. Let me get some chairs."

"I won't need one. I'm sticking my feet in the water to cool off."

"I'll join you."

They took off boots and sandals, then rolled up their jeans and sat on the edge, feet on the top step, food between them.

"If I close my eyes I can imagine that I'm on a picnic at a lake. That's on my bucket list, too."

"Wait a minute." Bryce looked seriously shocked behind his mirrored sunglasses. "You've never been on a picnic or to the lake?"

"Either. Neither. Whatever word I'm supposed to use." Kylie was seriously tempted to ask for a trip to buy a bathing suit and take the rest of the night to float.

"I have problems believing that." He shook his head and ate another chicken strip.

"I've eaten outside plenty of times. If you can call what I did back when I was modeling eating. We had photo shoots outdoors and I did plenty of rolling around in the surf at a beach. But never a family picnic or camping or riding bicycles… nothing like that."

"That's rough."

"Don't feel sorry for me. My job took me around the world more than a dozen times. I have some fantastic memories. Especially of the people I met and how gracious fans were."

"Now, you've got me on that one. I flew to Oklahoma City a couple of times. Driven to the surrounding five-state area a lot, but that's about it. Went to school here. My parents took off all the time, but I was the kid who preferred to stay home."

"You haven't traveled at all?"

"Well, I wouldn't say that. Texas is a pretty big place and I travel all over. I worked with DPS before landing this job." He must have noticed her blank stare. "Sort of like the state highway patrol. The Department of Public Safety is the division that the Rangers operate under since 1935. I can't think of anybody who didn't serve there before becoming a Ranger."

"I didn't even know how to drive a car until I married Xander. I never needed to learn before that. When I stole that Cadillac, I didn't have a license. I was horrified I'd have an accident and have to call someone to find me."

"So if you've never been on a picnic at a lake, I guess you've never gone skinny-dipping." He hung his glasses on the side of his boot.

"Of course not. I got paid to skinny-dip in the surf, though. That day was so cold." She shot him a fake shocked look and then splashed water his direction.

"Keep that up and you'll find out what it's like to be thrown into the pool."

"Been there. Done that." She decided to live dangerously and splash him again.

"Keep it up, Kylie. I live for revenge…at least where the pool is concerned. Last summer my nephew learned pretty quick how ruthless I can be and he's only seven."

"You have a nephew?"

"Four of them now. Each brother has one and my sister has two."

"That must be nice."

"At least for my parents. I get a lot of digital pictures. Oh, I almost forgot. I bought you a cell this afternoon. It's in the truck. Want me to get it?"

"But I don't need a phone."

"Fred and I disagree."

He stood on the first step, ankle deep in water. The compulsion to push him was overwhelming. She rose slightly and pushed against his hard abs almost as if he'd expected her to. He fell into the pool and she hoped his phone wasn't in his pocket. That would be dreadful. Nothing else that had happened mattered at that particular moment. He rocketed from the bottom of the pool and snatched her ankles.

Getting her wet wasn't a pull and dunk. His hand tickled the bottom of her feet until she was laughing so hard she couldn't breathe. Then he inched her under as she held on to the side of the pool. Then he held on to her waist as she surfaced.

"Oh, no you don't. I told you, I take my revenge seriously."

She went under to escape his grasp, but it didn't last long. They bounced around in the shallow end, taking turns coming up for air and darting back under. They slowed a little and were suddenly face-to-face.

"If we were kids my mother would be yelling to quit before someone got hurt," he said, out of breath.

Or at least acting like he was.

"Good thing we aren't kids then."

The heat of the sun and crispness of the water felt good, but she remembered the kiss from the bus. His mouth came closer to hers and she closed her eyes, letting him take her back to that awesome sensation.

No hesitation this time or wondering what his intentions were. She rested her arms on his shoulders and parted her lips. He whooshed her through the water, pulling her body into his. Every muscle was outlined and defined by the cotton. And each one of them was pressed against her.

The water didn't cool them down. The more they kissed, the hotter she got. The pool should have been bubbling. He lifted her in the water to have access to her neck, pushing her outer shirt off one shoulder.

She should stop him. She couldn't take it off… but it felt so good to be touched, to have his teeth nip at her skin, to feel again. She returned the action, tugging at his buttons and pushing his green shirt out of the way.

Mouths back together, it was hard to kiss through the smiles and playfulness, but he did. He wrapped his arms around her and took her below the water, kissing as long as she could hold her breath. When they came up, he caught the back of her long-sleeve shirt and pulled it free as she got away.

Without that protection, she was lost. Her sleeveless tank wouldn't cover the ugly flesh on her left arm. She swam away from Bryce, slicked back her hair and dipped her shoulders below the water.

With her right hand, she waved at Bryce as he set her shirt on the side of the pool tile. "Hey, I need that back."

"It'll be easier to swim without it. In fact, we

should take off our jeans, too. My wallet is probably ruined. So what? Won't be the first time."

"No, really, I need my shirt back please."

"Okay." He looked a little confused.

Probably because of the anxiousness in her voice. There was panic there, but as long as he gave her the shirt back, she'd be fine.

"Thanks." She reached out, keeping the scarred side of her body away from him. "Time to get out. No more games."

BRYCE COULD ONLY watch as Kylie turned away and struggled to get her shirt back on. As soon as she had her left arm through the sleeve she was hightailing it out of the water. Game time was definitely over.

Picking up their leftovers, she stuffed everything back into the bag. She slung the string of her bag across her shoulder and walked to the back door, dripping.

He followed. "Why are you so worried about me seeing the scars? I've seen wounds before. You can relax around here."

"I can't relax anywhere. Sorry. Can we just go inside? It's getting late."

The keys were still in the truck along with his cell and her new cell. She stood on the back patio, visibly shivering in the blazing July sun. He wiped the water running into his eyes away.

It was important for him to show her she didn't have to be afraid.

Time he didn't have. That's what he needed. Or maybe to have become a part of her life in a different month or year. But he was stuck with today. Stuck in the timeline where someone was trying to kill her.

"I'll grab your travel bag. You'll want your clothes."

He needed a minute to cool off, just leaning against the side of the truck. At the moment he doubted he could get his jeans off without ripping them with scissors. And that might be a little dangerous until all his parts calmed down.

With the bag hanging on the French door handle, she had stopped shaking and was wringing the water from her shirt. Then her hair.

Beautiful. She was just…beautiful.

Of course, she knew it. The whole world knew it. She'd been a model for more than half her life and didn't need to hear it from him. But he'd yearned to say it since he'd first met her. Natural beauty that came from deep within her soul. No scars would change that.

Bag in hand, he put the key in the lock, opened the door and they were both hit with a blast of cold air. "Want a towel or to make a run for it?"

"I'll follow you."

He darted forward and was halfway up the stairs when he realized she wasn't behind him.

She'd stopped to turn the dead bolt. He pretended like he hadn't seen her, slowing his pace. She caught up with him and at the top of the stairs he dropped her small case in the guest room and grabbed extra towels from the cabinet in the bath.

"Are you sure you're not married?"

"Yeah, pretty sure."

"Your place doesn't look like a bachelor lives here."

Bryce shrugged as if he was indifferent. "I have my mom to thank for that. She hired a decorator before they'd come to visit. Told me she was too old to sleep on an air mattress or eat off a paper plate."

Kylie laughed and was still laughing when she locked the door.

Showering eased some of the tension his body had built up, but not all of it. He put away the leftovers while she used the hair dryer. Back in a tank and a light long-sleeve shirt, she looked more relaxed when she came downstairs.

She packed her wet clothes in a plastic bag insisting she wasn't staying the night with him. But then started washing a load of towels she'd used.

While he showed her where things were, it was close quarters in the laundry room. There was an electric current between him and Kylie. Each time he passed close to her he wanted to touch. When he finally did, he might as well have stuck a screwdriver into an outlet. She jumped away from him so fast he wondered if those kisses had affected her in a different way.

"Coffee?"

"Sure. I need to warm up while we talk about this great plan of yours."

"Oh, yeah."

"There is a plan? You weren't lying to get me to come home with you?"

"No. I mean yes, there is. Fred's already set parts of it in motion." He backed out of the room as fast as he could, tripping on a laundry basket. "Why don't you start and tell me what happened with the judge."

"I'm sure you heard it online or somewhere that they dismissed all the charges, along with my protection detail. I'm surprised that you were sent after me to see if I'd cooperate again. The judge was pretty clear…" She slowed to a stop. "There's something you're not telling me."

There was a lot he wasn't telling, but she needed to know it wasn't official. There'd be no safety net other than the people of Hico.

"I guess I should start by letting you know I was officially suspended this morning, but that Major Parker told me this was the only way we could help."

"So you have his unofficial blessing to put together a plan? How's that supposed to help?"

"Since most of Hico will be in on the plan, the

state of Texas probably shouldn't be liable if something goes wrong."

"There's one major flaw in whatever your plan is. I'm not going back to Hico. I refuse to put all the people I hold dear in danger like that. And don't even bother telling me that Xander isn't a threat. He ambushed me with the judge's help and said he wanted his car back among other things."

"How did he ambush you?"

"The judge invited me into his office. He said he wanted to talk about—I don't remember. Xander was inside and the judge didn't bother staying."

Bryce wanted to find the judge and make him pay for that. But he also wanted to show Kylie he could protect her. But Kylie closed herself off. It wasn't the first time she'd reacted that way. This time he had a reason—Xander. He wanted two things for Kylie. First to not hide behind her clothes and the second was to not be afraid of the world.

"You okay?"

"Just great. At least I was while I was sitting on that bus putting a safe distance away from my friends. Are you ready to tell me what you're doing?"

"It won't work without you, Kylie." He wanted to hold her, to comfort her. "And you might think you're protecting everyone by running away, but consider a couple of things. Friends don't walk away from friendships. And then there's your ex. He assumes you've hidden the Cadillac in Hico somewhere. Your friends won't be safe until we put Xander behind bars."

Chapter Thirteen

Bryce was going to set a trap for her ex. He was determined to do it without the help of any law enforcement sanction or backup. He wanted her help.

And she didn't think he was crazy.

Or maybe she was just as crazy as he was for wanting to believe it might work.

"You've sort of hinted at this before Bryce. But what if you coming to Hico alerted someone? Then they came searching for me and the car."

"I have thought about that scenario more than once in the past week." Bryce rubbed his chin with both hands. "The plan will work. We'll catch whoever shot up your house. You'll be safe."

His house was decorated as if he'd been married and his wife hated the place. There weren't any real traces of Bryce. No pictures of family, only a rare landscape photograph hung on the wall. The color choice was neutral...everywhere neutral. There wasn't even a sport trophy in the game room where they were sitting.

"I'm changing the subject, Bryce. You said your mother hired a decorator. Did they consult you at all?"

"To make her happy I said she could do what she wanted. I don't spend much time anywhere except this room and the bedroom."

"I can understand why. It's so…"

"Bleak? Old? Stuffy?"

"I was going to say beige."

"Are you okay with the plan, Kylie?" Bryce licked chicken from his fingers then wiped them in a napkin.

There was nothing special about it. Nothing meant to be provocative. So why were her insides fluttering with excitement? He leaned forward on a knee, sort of expecting an answer. What had he asked?

"I, ah…I'm willing to give it a try. I don't know if it will work, but I don't want to leave Hico. I need a life. Not…"

"Beige."

They laughed awkwardly. "Right. It's time to live some bright bold colors."

As long as it wasn't red, but she wouldn't say that out loud. He didn't need to wonder about her commitment to his plan. At least he had one.

He was finishing up another round of chicken. She'd passed on seconds but had nibbled on a roll.

She'd gotten to the point that thinking wasn't really helping. A weird sensation of the more she tried, the fewer thoughts were actually in her mind.

"It's bothering me that Xander didn't act like he knew where the car was located. Am I missing something?"

"Fred disconnected the GPS locator and moved it. No one but him knows where it is."

"But Xander reacted like he hadn't known I was the one who stole the car at all."

"Interesting." Bryce's jaw muscles flexed.

"Don't agree with me and just blow off my opinion. I know what I'm talking about. I know what he said."

"No, sorry. I'm thinking it's a legitimate theory. Fred said he hadn't connected the charger until this last week. So whoever had the GPS on the car might have just realized it was on."

"I am totally lost. Explain it to me."

She was lost. But mainly at the thought that someone besides her ex-husband hated her so much.

"Say someone—Xander or an unknown—wanted the car. Let's say they've been looking for you or waiting on you to surface."

"I don't see why, but okay."

"Kylie, I've been looking for you for three years because the state was interested."

"Why? I don't understand."

"The state has been working on a case against the Tenoreno family for a decade. This is the closest they've gotten to bringing their crime syndicate down. You were a piece of the puzzle." He scratched his chin, thinking.

"A missing piece."

"Exactly. So when the picture of you surfaced, I came to check it out. It hasn't been a secret that the state wanted to find you. We didn't broadcast that we had, but we didn't keep it a secret either."

"So it really is quite possible that you alerted someone that I was alive and living in Hico." The wonder of it blew her away, because no one believed that she didn't have a clue about the Tenoreno family's business. Even after all this time… "So you think Xander is lying?"

"Maybe, but we have to be prepared that two different parties might be interested in the car. You know, I don't think whoever fired at us Saturday got to your house before us. So if they did follow me to Hico, then located the car, they still waited for instructions on how to proceed."

"How does that help?"

"The men shooting at us were following orders…not giving them." He nodded his head as if he'd had a breakthrough.

"Well that makes everything perfectly clear for me." She couldn't even laugh about it. Like her brain trying to think everything through to a conclusion and getting nowhere, it seemed her emotional bank was completely depleted, too.

"The plan is a basic one. We move the car back to your place and wait for them to show up. Whoever *they* are, we'll be ready."

"You, Fred and a few other Hico citizens."

"Fred spoke to the police officers and they're evacuating the homes. They'll be ready." He leaned back against the cushions again, more relaxed. "We didn't want to put you or anyone in danger."

"I don't think you're responsible for that particular mistake in my life."

Bryce smiled. "Maybe not. I will be if something goes wrong. The idea is to get to them before they get anywhere near you. That's it."

"And what if Xander or this mystery person doesn't show?"

"I'm thinking of one solution at a time." He leaned forward to pick up the remote. "I'll show you how to use this thing if you want to watch television. I have some stuff I need to take care of."

"Oh, then I'll call a cab to take me to a motel."

He scrunched up his face and cocked his head as though he hadn't heard her correctly. "There's a bedroom upstairs. I'm not spending the night at a hotel watching you sleep."

"I didn't ask you to."

"Kylie, do me this one favor and let's not argue

about where we're sleeping. We're safer here than at a motel. I have an alarm. Locks. Bolts. If I hear something, I have lots of protection in my gun safe."

Everything he named off made her feel more secure. She wouldn't let pride or whatever she was feeling put them in jeopardy. "I didn't want to be trouble."

"Will you please stay here?"

She nodded her head and saw lights in the yard. The pool lights reflected off the six-foot fence and she didn't have to imagine that it was prettier sitting next to it. "Now I wish I'd packed my bathing suit."

"Suits are always optional. You could mark skinny-dipping off your bucket list." He smiled overly wide like an emoticon.

"But it's not on *my* bucket list. Driving through the fall leaves in New England…now *that's* on my list."

"Shame. I could help you cross off something tonight, right now."

He was so cute. But skinny-dipping meant no coverage. She tugged the light long-sleeve shirt into a more comfortable position.

"If you have to work, I guess I should just go on up, then."

"I didn't say work. I was suspended, remember?"

"How could I forget since I was the reason?"

"I need some research. I'm not working for anyone but you. So what else is on your bucket list? Not seeing the world. You've done that several times."

"Having a dog, for one."

"That's cool."

"Really? Most people would think it's too simple."

"Who said simple things couldn't make a bucket list?" Bryce's arm was along the back of the couch and touched her. "I'd like a reason to take a day off and lay around that pool. Maybe meet my neighbors. Have a barbecue. Is getting to a lake picnic on your top ten?"

She forced herself not to react to the simple brush of his finger along her shirt. Everything about the evening had been casual. She wanted to keep it that way. But her insides were doing that flutter thing again. Or maybe they'd never stopped.

"I guess it should be. Mine is really silly. Let's change the subject. I'll watch a movie if you watch it, too."

He grabbed her hand as she reached for the remote.

Maybe they shouldn't be relaxing at all. It was all quite possible everything was about to go to hell in a handbasket or in a 1964 fully restored shiny black Cadillac convertible.

"This thing's crazy. Trust me with the remote?"

"We aren't watching football, right?"

"Not this time of year. What do you like? Suspense, drama, comedy—"

He was looking at the cable guide. "I don't think I could take *The Fugitive* or anything like that. And I'm not too sure comedy would work."

"*King Kong*?" He looked at her and moved on to the next one. "Classic John Wayne. You've got to like John Wayne?"

"All right."

"You don't sound very enthusiastic."

"I just saw this one three weeks ago."

"Then we keep flipping."

"No, Bryce, it's okay. Really. Oh wait, go back." She flipped her fingers until he returned to the right channel. "Is that Fred Astaire? Would you mind if we watched that? I've been on an old movie kick. I was going to set my DVR but—"

"But everything in your house was shredded. I remember."

He leaned back against the couch. "Want popcorn or soda? Maybe a beer?"

"I'm good, thanks."

Bryce leaned his head back on the cushion. Kylie expected him to be snoring before the first dance number. But she didn't mind. Sitting here like two normal adults was ridiculously soothing. And exactly what she needed.

She loved the idea of normal.

That was on her bucket list, too.

It wasn't long and *The End* rolled across the screen. Bryce had slept through the entire movie. She wanted to turn off the TV and tried but pushed the wrong button in the dark. A DVD began playing and before she could click it off a THX sound check played at practically the loudest level available.

BRYCE SHOT OFF the couch, eyes wide open, realizing exactly what had happened. "Middle top turns everything off."

Kylie pushed the remote but handed it off to him. It took him a second or two. Whatever she'd attempted in the dark had switched a different electronic device on instead of cutting everything off.

"I didn't mean to wake you up, but I had no idea a remote could be so complicated."

"Universal remote." He wiped the sleep from his eyes. "Did you enjoy the movie? Sorry I sort of passed out. Guess our swim had me more tired than I realized. Did I snore?"

She shook her head and yawned. "You didn't, but I might if I stay up any later. And yes, the movie was great. Fred and Ginger—what's not to love?"

"All the dancing?"

"You don't like to dance? That's another thing on my list. I want to learn how to waltz properly."

"All right." He began clicking through the

music stored in his system. "I'm sure I put something that had a three-quarter time beat… Mom's playlist. That's it."

He scrolled through and found the perfect song, put it on Repeat and opened his arms.

"What's this?" She looked baffled.

"'Waltz Across Texas.' That's how you waltz with boots on."

"We're both barefoot, Bryce." Her hands were on her hips, the flowy shirt that hid her skin pushed behind them. Skinny jeans hugged her long legs and the dark T-shirt clung to her, outlining perfect-sized breasts and waistline.

"Perfect." *In more way than one.* He set a hand on her hip and held his palm open for her to drop hers onto. "Barefoot is how I learned."

"What do I do?"

"Follow my lead. My granddad told me to keep the lady's foot between mine and hold her close. Do you mind?" He didn't wait for permission, the song played again and he tugged her to fit against him. "Now don't get any ideas about throwing me to the floor."

Kylie laughed for the first time since the pool. She might be tall, but she was really a tiny thing.

Kylie tried to drop her chin and look at their feet.

"Chin up and trust me, darlin'. I know where I'm going."

He led her around to the back of the couch,

keeping them in a tight square. He counted off the three beats in his head. She let him lead completely as if she'd never attempted a waltz before. Had she?

Maybe she had and he'd misinterpreted? "I like these words."

"My grandparents danced to this at least once a week when I was young." *One, two, three. One, two, three.* He needed to keep this right and not mess up. "If it wasn't the first song they danced to, it was the last one. They even played it at their funerals."

"It's nice that you have that to remember, but it's a little sad."

"Dancing made them happy. They passed it on to all of us." His fingers flexed across her back, anxious to get her even closer.

She tipped her head back and stopped moving her feet. "Wait a second, you just said that the thing wrong with the movie was all the dancing."

"Watching other people dance isn't the same as holding a woman in your arms." He secured his arm tighter around her, curled her fingers within his.

She rested her head on his shoulder, her warm breath was calm and regular across his skin. Lucky she couldn't feel his, which was getting more excited with each step. He pulled her closer still and gently nudged his knee between hers to keep them locked together in the waltz box.

Dancing together was close and intimate behind his couch and he felt the heat. He wanted to kiss Kylie, but the repeating voice of Tex Ritter was beginning to wear a little on the mood. Instead, he twirled them close to the amplifier and selected Random.

Mistake. The beat changed to something from the '70s.

"That was lovely, but this…" Her hands went to his shoulders, not pushing, just ready to be released. "I can dance to on my own."

Bryce went to the next song and wrapped her hand back in his, admiring the strength he felt in the slender aikido-filled defense weapons. He hugged her, swaying to the soft band music from the '40s. Kept her close to him through the next '60s song with a faster tempo. Then encouraged her head to rest on his shoulder when Frankie Valli sang "You're just too good to be true."

"You sing pretty good."

"I didn't realize I was." He didn't sing for anyone. It gave him a weird feeling. He hadn't even played drums in high school because he didn't like to perform.

Barefoot. Three feet of carpet either direction. Hand in hand. This time when he kissed her it was different. The edge of not knowing what he wanted was gone. He knew exactly.

Kylie.

Chapter Fourteen

Daniel Rosco was on his back in coveralls wheeling himself under a 1976 Trans Am. He was restoring it himself. The tediousness of working and cleaning every part on the engine was the only thing that calmed him.

As a child, his mother would send him out here when she saw him overly anxious. The garage had been immaculately clean and he'd yearned to get grease on his hands. Paco Valdez had been their driver back then. He'd taught him a lot about engines, but most of Daniel's knowledge came from research and intuition.

Paco was gone now. He'd been gone many more years than his mother or father, who had both been murdered in the past six months. *Murdered! Taken out. Gotten out of the way.*

It wasn't something he hadn't thought about doing himself…especially with his father. He didn't like that the decision had been taken out of his hands. He knew the man responsible. He'd once called him his close friend in spite of the rivalries and competition between their families.

Xander would suffer for standing by and letting his father execute his sweet momma. But he'd slit the throat of the bastard himself for ordering the assassin who left his father to rot in the desert.

Xander's days were numbered. And now that he knew where the flash drive was located… It was just a matter of time before all his plans became reality.

"Boss?"

Daniel set his wrench on his chest and rolled the creeper from under the car, wiping his hands on an oily rag that put more dirt on them than took off. He carefully placed the wrench among the other well-used tools. All arranged precisely in the order he expected to use them.

Lennon waited. He knew not to ask mundane questions like what Daniel was doing. Otherwise the wrench might land against his head instead of being replaced on the towel.

"Do you have him?" He stood, hopping to his feet, feeling like a teenager instead of someone approaching thirty.

"Yes, sir, but Xander Tenoreno is here to see you."

"Interesting. I didn't expect him until I had the package. How close are we to that detail?"

"The model's house is being watched. The local authorities don't know we're already in place."

"Excellent. Send in Xander. I'm excited to hear what he has to say to me." His back was to the door when Xander entered, but he could see his rival in the small mirror above the sink.

"I guess you know why I'm here. The man you had spying on me said your hired thugs put on quite a show. What the hell were you thinking?"

"The package will be in my possession within twenty-four hours." Daniel dried his hands and shrugged out of his coveralls, tying the arms around his waist. "Then our deal is off."

"You hired men behind my back to take care of our problem. I thought we had a partnership."

"You should have told me your ex had the drive. Trust runs both ways...friend."

"What even makes you think the drive is still in the Cadillac? Or that you beat me to it? Do you think I would have left it with Sissy all these years?"

"You don't have it." He took the other man's measure, gauging how far to push him. "Just as I knew you did then...you don't have it now."

"What about the partnership between the families? Are we going back to square one, fighting for the scraps that the Mexican cartel will leave?"

They moved around each other, opposite points on a circle they were walking.

"My father was an old man, willing to go into

business with yours, and look what it got him. Dead. I'm not old and I'm no longer willing to step aside. I think we both know why."

"Sissy doesn't have any idea what's hidden in the car. If she had the information she would have used it long before now or thrown it in my face yesterday."

Daniel had control over his body. He didn't act concerned at all.

"I wondered if you'd seen her. I suppose you made arrangements with the authorities." Daniel dropped his hand on Xander's shoulder, stopping their dance around each other. "It amazes me you believe that in all these years she never looked at the drive."

"You aren't going to kill her until we know for certain." Xander knocked Daniel's hands aside.

"Of course I am." He moved to the wall of screwdrivers and files, but didn't expect to use them. This was his garage with his men stationed all around.

"I should have killed you years ago, Daniel. But we were friends. I thought we had a plan to take everything from our fathers. Telling you of the missing Cadillac was a big mistake on my part. But it's been your impatience that led prosecutors to my ex-wife. It was your impatience that has involved the authorities and made the entire situation more important. I doubt they'll walk away anytime soon."

"You aren't claiming any responsibility for not finding her during the past five years? If you'd handled this correctly to begin with—"

"No one could have known it was Sissy who stole the car." Xander said matter-of-factly. "I'll deal with it. Back away, Daniel, before you destroy everything we've worked for."

Xander turned to leave.

Daniel's hand closed around the handle of a screwdriver. It could have been thrown like a knife. But…he wanted Xander alive to witness the Tenoreno empire fall. Old-fashioned, yes. What could he say? He enjoyed theatrics. Maybe he'd seen *The Godfather* too many times.

"You go through with your plans in Hico," Xander said at the door, "and we'll have to take extreme measures."

"Are you threatening me?"

The death in Xander's look might have frightened him when he was younger. Daniel knew the look well. He practiced it. He lived it.

Tenoreno sauntered away, thinking he had the upper hand. Seconds later, Daniel's right-hand man—everyone in this business had one—stood in the open doorway ready for the next order. Daniel gestured to send the man in.

"Let's get this over with, Lennon."

The man who had lost track of Xander's ex-wife was thrown through the garage door and left alone with Daniel. Feeling like a man with power, he sat on the workbench stool and retrieved a pistol. He spun, then opened the chamber very dramatically.

"I've got to let people know what happens to men who don't follow my orders."

"I'm sorry, Mr. Rosco, but I didn't know he was going to take her off the bus."

"I. Don't. Care." He dropped a bullet from a chamber for emphasis of each word. Then two more. The theatrics was just that. Fun. Nobody was there to witness the murder. It was just drama and made him feel like the boss. He'd seen his father go through this ritual at least half a dozen times before he was fifteen.

With one bullet remaining, Daniel handed him the pistol.

"This is simple. Pull the trigger on yourself and we're even. Pull it on me and every person you love dies."

The explosion was expected. It was the man's only choice after all was said and done. Lennon came through the door, a moment of wonder wiped from his face as soon as it appeared.

"Sorry about the mess, Lennon. We should have used the drop cloth. Get the body disposed of and send five hundred to his family."

Daniel was tempted again to take care of Sissy himself. He'd only met her a couple of times while she'd been married to Xander. But there was too much heat near her at the moment to make that possible. The men he'd hired couldn't be traced back to him. It was better to stay clear and let them handle it.

They had nothing to lose and soon the little town of Hico would look like a war-trodden wreck. "Who knows? Maybe Xander will want to intervene and get stuck in the middle of it. One can always hope."

Chapter Fifteen

Perfectly shaped lips, effortlessly pink without artificial color. Eyes a beautiful shade of blue with a little definition. Blue? Great detective skills. She'd been wearing dark-colored contacts until today. Bryce left Kylie's lips, skimming her cheek then her jawline to whisper in her ear as he passed it.

"You ready to head upstairs?"

"Why, Mr. Johnson, are you asking me what I think you're asking me?" She skimmed his lips, then sucked his bottom lip between her teeth. "Never going to happen."

He would have believed her if she'd pulled away. Or maybe even if she'd said the "never" with a bounce in her voice. But she hadn't. Her voice was full of sadness—not fright like that afternoon—just sadness and regret.

"I've been afraid to tell you," he whispered, searching her eyes and seeing the hunger he felt. "I think—"

He couldn't blink, connected as he was to her emotional pain.

"Don't think that you know me, Bryce. If you've been searching for Sissy Jorgenson... Well, she died five years ago. I told you that. I have the scars to prove it. I'm not afraid of them, but I don't share that part of me with anyone. They remind me every day that I was given a second chance. Those shots took away a career, security, my friends. But they gave me a family in Hico that I couldn't fully appreciate until this week. For that I'll always be grateful to you."

She turned to leave, slowly. Hesitating. Letting him keep her fingers secured inside his hand.

"Let me ask you a simple question."

"What?"

"Do you *want* to go upstairs with me?"

"There's nothing simple about that question." Her chin dropped to her chest, her free hand covered her eyes.

"Sure there is. I know my answer. And I think I know yours." He pulled her back to him and devoured her mouth. She allowed him access to the curve of her neck, the soft skin across her collarbone.

Answering his invitation without words. Her hands were on his hips bringing him closer and harder against her. Their bodies rocked against each other when Deep Purple's "Smoke on the

Water" shot through the speakers. Her tongue danced inside his mouth, darting, demanding.

She was in charge of their fate. And he kept his hands above his head to prove it to her. He told himself he could walk away if she changed her mind. But he sure as hell didn't want to.

She pushed at his T-shirt. Since his hands were in the air, practically above his head, he reached to his shoulders and pulled it free. Her mouth left his, pressing against his chest. Teasing with a mixture of a lick with the tip of her tongue and a playful bite. She worked her way down, her short nails scraping lightly until they reached the top of his zipper, then outlined his erection underneath.

"Let's go," he whispered when she unbuttoned his fly.

"What's wrong with here?" Her fingers drew circles on his abs.

"Kylie." He shook his head, then caught the look in her eyes.

It was back, the fright that he'd seen when her shirt came off.

"I like it right here," she whispered trying to sink to her knees.

He slid his hands to her elbows, stopping her. "I'm not treating our first time together like we're teenagers looking for a fast thrill in a game room. We're not only too old for that, we deserve better."

Dusting her hands like she was done, she hurried away. "Fine. This is all I have, Bryce. All I can do."

He touched her shoulder and she stopped. Did she want him to change her mind? Show her how much he cared about her? "If it were me... If our positions were reversed, and I was the one with scars. What would you do right now, Kylie? Would you let me run away? Continue to be afraid?"

She covered her face. "I am afraid."

He could barely hear her. He asked just as quietly, "Of me?"

"Strangely enough, no. But yes, maybe of you most of all."

"I don't understand."

Kylie faced him, cupping his cheeks, using a thumb to entice his lips—whether that was her intention or not.

"You've been looking for Sissy. I've seen that desire before from the men who admired her beauty. I'm afraid that you'll be—"

"Be what?"

"Disappointed, Bryce. You're going to be disappointed and never look at me like that again." She gulped, holding back tears.

He pulled her in close again, this time for comfort. He wanted to tell her it wasn't true, but something told him to just be quiet. Let her cry. He hated that she was afraid, but there was a kernel of hope buried in there...

She not only wanted him…she didn't want him to just go away after they made love?

He wanted that, too. He wanted a relationship. And she was wrong—Sissy had been a young girl of the world. He was falling for the woman from a small town.

Kylie was warm against his chest. Tiny but not frail. Crying, but catching her breath. He was glad to hold her and wait, trying to form the words he wanted to say.

"Sweetheart, I'm not the person you're afraid of. I have no intention of walking away from you anytime soon. Believe me when I tell you that I have a pretty good imagination about what you look like, and yeah, I saw a lot of your modeling career photos. But none of that will ever compare to the real thing. You have to trust me a little."

"I do, but—I don't know how to get past this."

"Hell, you don't want me to see anything? Just blindfold me." He was joking. She knew he was joking, right?

When he saw the relief on her face, he knew he shouldn't be joking. It was the solution she needed and might be a little fun at the same time. No, this was serious.

"It'll probably kill me, but we'll move at whatever pace you need. Hands wherever you want them." He splayed them, stuck them behind his back, then extended his right. "Deal?"

"Deal." She took it and shook, but quickly grasped his face and kissed him.

And kept kissing him until her hands were moving up his back and it was as though their foreplay hadn't been interrupted. He wanted the first time to be special, but he'd never forget this woman or what was about to happen.

"Dish towel or necktie?" he asked when she nibbled on his neck.

"Tie, I think I'll get a better knot."

"Good."

As tall as she was she still weighed nothing. He picked her up and bolted up the stairs. He bounced her onto the king bed and pulled dress ties from the closet. Kylie had the comforter and top sheet thrown to the side. She was sitting on her knees in the middle, plumping pillows.

He gave her a choice of two ties he never wore. She pulled the one decorated with four-leaf clovers, sliding it across his palm.

Yeah, he felt pretty darn lucky already.

"You know you don't have to do this, Bryce."

"Believe me. That's no longer an option. I'll be right back."

The package of condoms had been in the cabinet for a while. He took two, just in case, and dropped them on the nightstand next to the bed.

"Feeling ambitious?" she asked moving to the edge.

"More like prepared."

"So how does this work?" She pulled the tie from one hand to the other.

A simple gesture that was anything other than innocent. It fired his imagination. On any other day he could keep his pants on to hold himself back. This one he had to dig deep to find the strength.

All he could do was swallow hard and shrug. "You're running the show."

A split-second look of uncertainty, then the playful Kylie stood and draped the tie around his neck. "I guess I am."

His body thrummed as she slowly ran her hands over his skin again, making him tense each time she dropped a finger down the edge of his jeans. The button was already undone. Just when he thought she'd forgotten about blindfolding him, she backed up and gestured for him to turn around.

Anticipation had his heart racing and pumping the blood through his body until he was almost jittery. And she'd done nothing but touch him. The tie slid to his back, looped around his neck. He closed his eyes, hearing the bed move.

Kylie positioned his blindfold, pulling it tight against his eyelids. She must have been standing on the bed because her lips and teeth tugged at the skin on the back of his neck and across his shoulders.

She didn't ask if it was too snug. It didn't matter if it was. He couldn't object or she might lose her nerve. *He* wouldn't. He wanted her, wanted them together. But more than that, he wanted to give her the confidence to live again.

And making love was part of living.

There was more rustling behind him. The dark surrounding him was absolute. He turned his head, but could only imagine that Kylie was removing her clothes.

"Time to get rid of that denim you're wearing." She patted his butt like a teammate.

"You're not going to help?"

"I think you can manage that in the dark. But here."

Reaching around him, the back of her cooled fingers dipped against his skin, holding his jeans at the top of his zipper. Before he could fully suck in his surprised breath, she'd playfully outlined his erection, then unzipped.

Those same knuckles stroked him again through the last layer of cotton. He reached for the jeans at his hips and she slapped his hands away.

"I changed my mind. This is temptingly fun."

"Or cruel."

"It was your idea. Want me to stop?" She stroked him again, slower this time.

He was breathing through his teeth. He couldn't help it. He shook his head and felt his jaw popping as the intense pleasure of her touch tightened every muscle in his body...*every* muscle.

She tugged the jeans down…one side, then the other. Back and forth a couple of times until they could slide down his legs. He was grateful to step out of them and wished she'd tugged his last bit of clothing along with them.

She slowly spun him around and checked the blindfold. It was still tight. He didn't know what to do with his hands, so he laced his fingers together and rested them on top of his head.

Kylie giggled.

"Having fun?" he asked.

"Not that I would want them or anything, but I imagined handcuffs for a second. I mean…you are standing like you're under arrest."

"Search away."

Vulnerable and uncertain—understatements for the way he felt. The darkness changed his expectations. He listened, trying to picture what she was doing based on the sound. He concentrated on her movements and anticipated every touch. He was still caught off guard when the bed moved and he was suddenly propelled to his back.

"You'll have to scoot to the middle on your own."

He did.

"I kind of like your hands where they are." Her nails created a trail of sensation down his side and across his belly, their tips skirted under the elastic. Teasing yet again.

He took a pillow from above his head and

gripped it with both of his hands. His concentration was split between the delicious trace of provocativeness and keeping his word to only do what she wanted, when she said so.

The light skimming across his skin with fingers and lips and bra silk had him bringing the pillow on top of his face. It lasted the barest of moments as Kylie extended her body over his and uncovered him.

Kissing. Nipping. Fully. Sensually. Completely. He was running out of ways to think about it. He was running out of the willpower to hold back.

"Honey, if you don't let me touch you soon…"

"Patience," she whispered tugging on his earlobe with her teeth.

He concentrated on her breasts rubbing across his chest, still covered by their satin cage. His fingers contracted as he envisioned them in his hands. Kylie's mouth substituted for her nipples. She pulled back and he went with her, rising off the bed as she sat across his lap.

He groaned with the pressure. The knowledge that at some point he'd be surrounded by her had him dropping like a hard rock back to the mattress. Groaning yet again.

"Kylie." He was breathing hard as though he'd run a marathon and they hadn't really begun yet. "Sweetheart, you…are you doing okay?"

As far as he could tell she was fine. He wanted more right then. He swallowed hard, grabbing the sheets under his hands as she tugged his underwear down his legs. He couldn't see but felt himself come to attention.

So aware of everything around him, he heard the cloth hit the carpet. Heard the short intake of breath as Kylie saw him for the first time. Felt the hesitation in her fingers as she explored more of his body.

Bryce was at his limit. Her tentative kiss was his undoing.

He must have died at that point, because he was definitely in heaven.

KYLIE WAS ENJOYING the small bit of torture she was putting Bryce through. But there was only so much she could manage without torturing herself.

Her desire had been almost unmanageable when they'd had all their clothes on. Now that his were off… He was such a gorgeous man. The sunburn from the weekend before had turned brown. The pale color from his waist down might have been comical if he wasn't so…impressive.

No. There wasn't anything funny about the way he made her want him. All he had to do was lie there and her body trembled.

Aching for him was the easy part.

Was it fair to keep him blindfolded? Literally in the dark where her body was concerned. She leaned forward to remove the lucky tie. Her bra skimmed his chest and another genuine groan escaped from Bryce. She wanted to release him, have him take a turn torturing her with touches and kisses and exploration.

But she just couldn't.

Instead, she used the silk of her underwear, sliding against him until his head shook side to side.

"Dammit, Kylie. Please let me touch you." One of his hands twisted the pillow into a ball, the other twisted in the sheet at their sides. "I'm being honest, sweetheart. This is getting hard."

A burst of laughter escaped. "I am so sorry."

He moaned. "Great balls of fire, I didn't mean that the way it sounded." His ab muscles tightened as he chuckled when she laughed more. "Shoot, I didn't mean *that* either."

"It's my fault. I know I'm not supposed to laugh."

"Why the hell not?"

"Well, won't it sort of deflate your ego?"

"Honey, there's nothing deflating there." He flexed under her.

He was right…nothing was deflating. She kissed him with all her confidence restored. She turned to her side, tugging him on top of her. She was ready. She had to give him a chance.

"Okay."

"Okay I can take the blindfold off, okay?" His hand went to push it away.

Both her hands grabbed his, stopping him in time. "No. I meant that I was ready."

"You might be, but I haven't had my turn yet." He switched to his side, then to his knees. "It's your call, but don't you want me to take a turn?"

"You would have to…touch me."

"That you can count on." His hand skimmed from her stomach to the top of her bra. "You're still dressed?"

Straddling her, he tugged a little on her panties, replicating what she'd done to him. Shouldn't he put a pleasurable end to the need building even higher? Of course he could…but he wasn't.

He touched her like a blind man. Exploring every crevice of one leg and then the other without stirring what was between. Purposefully ignoring her and using his light coating of facial hair to tickle her behind her knees…and then farther.

When he latched on to her hips, his fingertips were so close to one of the scars she thought he glided across it. He touched her intimately, thoroughly, and suddenly she didn't care where he'd touched before.

"Relax, hon, breathe," he whispered.

Had she forgotten to breathe? She certainly hadn't forgotten to feel. Every infinitesimal brush where their skin met was on fire and ready to explode. Breathing she could handle if he would just take her…

Never completing the thought, she fell into a

moment of tense nothingness. And then again. She felt like crying for mercy until she realized his hand was on her scar.

The torn flesh was numb to her. No feeling had ever come back. She was both breathing hard from where Bryce had taken her moments ago and holding her breath because of what he'd say.

"Kylie? Is there a chance?" He touched the lucky clover tie. "Trust me."

Whether he really said those words right then or they echoed in her mind from earlier, she didn't know. But she did. She wanted to trust him with all of her and that meant letting him see the scars.

If he was repulsed so be it. But in her heart she knew Bryce was different. There was something in the way he looked into her eyes and understood.

Scooting away from him, she saw his shoulders droop in apparent defeat. He couldn't see that she was heading to him to remove his blindfold. He jerked in surprise when her hands touched his handsome face.

Once she'd pushed the tie onto his forehead, his eyes started to blink. She put her palm across them, keeping them closed before he could focus. They were face-to-face, knee to knee on his giant bed.

He took her hand in his, and kept his eyelids closed hiding the cinnamon brown beneath, but not the attention he gave her or his patience.

"You don't have to be afraid to take this next

step or to go the distance with me, Kylie." He cupped his chin with her hand and leaned into it, then kissed her palm. "I won't let you down. Promise."

It was time to share the last bit of herself.

"Open your eyes."

Chapter Sixteen

Bryce opened his eyes and Kylie turned on her left side. It was easier to hide. At least until he made a move to really look. She hadn't paid attention that the bedroom lights had been on, suddenly wishing she'd turned the brighter ones off.

No regrets now. She'd enjoyed looking at Bryce's body. She couldn't deny that most of her life had been around beautiful people and she knew how to appreciate the contours of his body.

She looked up at him, attempting not to be in a rush. Yet, her heart raced and the heat of his stare made her flush.

He gently nudged her to her back. "I imagined your bra as red."

"I don't own anything red. I hate that color."

"I'll remember that. The pink is sexy. Did the underwear match?"

She nodded, biting her lower lip. His grin disappeared when he noticed the healed wound above her hip. His fingers traced it. And like before, she felt his fingertip around the edge but not the actual scar.

"Where are the others?"

She pointed under her arm. "The jagged rip had never been repaired correctly."

"Why?"

"I didn't hang around the hospital longer than I had to. Especially after they pulled the protective detail. When it happened there wasn't time and when there was time, there was no money for a plastic surgeon."

He stretched out along her left, pulling her into the curve of his body. She felt so protected it hurt to realize how much she'd longed for it. He caressed both scars. Seriously caressed.

Over the years, she'd never imagined getting close to someone again. Never dreamed that she'd be intimate. Wondering how a lover would react had always been intertwined with her horrified repulsion.

"Your body was made for me to make love to it." Bryce spread his large hand across her tummy, then up again to her breast.

He teased the flesh at the edge of the satin. Feathery light caresses back and forth from her ear to thigh. Touches that almost said more, teasing her as much as she had him.

Propped on one elbow, he got her excited with one hand. She relaxed into his body and let him push the strap down over her shoulder. His lips and teeth nipped on her skin and then closer and closer to the flesh she wanted him to devour.

Bryce kissed until only skin was between them. Somehow the protection of her bra was gone as he twirled her nipple under his tongue. His movements had been subtle and delicate, then he moved on top of her, cupping both of her breasts into his hands.

His fingers found her last secret, the one she could hide under the bright pink satin. The most horrific reminder of all... He paused only for a second—if that long—raising himself on one arm and forcing her to meet his eyes.

"I've wanted to tell you this since I first met you in Hico." He dramatically paused, no smile, his brown eyes darting to every inch of her face. "You're too beautiful for words."

Kylie threw her arms around his neck, pulling him to her so their lips met. Their hips meshed together and they rocked in a frenzy. Bryce remembered the condom. She watched while his hands shook a little adjusting it into place.

Then they danced for real. A tempo that was faster than a waltz. What did someone call a dance that grew to a crashing crescendo? It didn't matter.

Kylie felt alive. In fact, she felt *everywhere*. The tips of her fingers and toes were electric. There was a buzzing in her ears as the world was blocked out and Bryce spun her out of control. And spun her again until he joined her.

The exhaustion was just like they'd danced the night away.

They lay tangled in each other's arms and legs. She was getting self-conscious and was moving to grab the sheet when Bryce's hand landed on her left breast. His fingers gently caressed the far side and the bullet's path.

"You survived, Kylie," he said into her shoulder. "There's nothing ugly in that."

Bryce was well on the way to another nap. Definitely a nap. She'd let him rest for a moment before she reached for that second package and let him twirl her on their private dance floor again.

The music was still playing downstairs. She heard it while trying not to cry at his simple, beautiful words. Trying not to fall in love with him a little more than she already was.

BRYCE WASN'T USED to eight hours of sleep. Hell, he wasn't used to six hours of sound sleep. The closer the Tenoreno murder trial had gotten, there'd rarely been a reason not to work late, or travel, or bring work home with him.

He was awake with the dawn and strategically getting out of bed without disturbing Kylie. He pulled on swimming trunks and did something rare. He swam laps. Short ones because the pool wasn't designed for that sort of thing, but laps nevertheless.

And during his time in the water he only had time to think. He cared about Kylie and didn't want her to return to Hico. There wasn't any logical reason for her not to. He knew she wouldn't stay away. How could he expect her to agree when all of her friends were going to such extremes setting the trap?

Yeah, she was the bait. But was bait necessary for this fishing expedition? He was an idiot for blabbing the plan before thinking it all the way through. He started the coffeemaker and grabbed a shower downstairs just in case she was still asleep.

There'd been no hesitation making love to him a second time. No hiding on her side or behind a bra. Just wanton sexual satisfaction for them both.

Was it? Not for him.

He didn't just care about Kylie helping with his plan. He cared about her. But he'd already known that.

"Good morning." She practically sang the words through a smile he hadn't seen since she'd told the kids he was buying pizza. "I smelled that coffee while I was in the shower. Is it strong?"

"Strong enough."

"As in standing a spoon in the cup and I should use some milk? Or is it actually drinkable?"

"Milk."

She opened cabinets like he had the first time after his mom had the place redone. Logically looking for coffee cups, closest to the coffeemaker. "Are you grumpy first thing every morning?"

"Not usually. I've been thinking." *And thinking. And thinking.*

She paused with the coffee carafe midair. "Trying to think of a reason for me not to be a part of your trap, I suppose."

"Yep."

"There's only one thing that will keep me out of Hico. Call the whole thing off." She poured two cups, then milk into one.

"I've weighed that option. If I call it off, you'll never be safe. But there is a chance if we go through with the Hico plan. It's up to you whether we take it." He was so mixed-up about what she should do. Had his mind shut down because they'd made love? He honestly didn't know which was better for her. Each plan carried its own set of risks. He didn't like either of them.

"I knew there was something I liked about you."

She set the cups down and was close enough for him to snag then pull into his lap. He didn't have to think long on whether to thoroughly kiss her. "Good morning." Man, oh man, he loved her lips.

"So there's a couple of things I like." She winked.

"Nothing I can say to change your mind? I'm not exaggerating about how dangerous it is."

"You were very clear about that when you were explaining and reminding me how close we came to being shot last weekend. I watched your eyes when the realization hit you that someone might get hurt. It's dangerous for everyone. Even you." She reached for the coffee, changed her mind and kissed him instead. "I know you'll take every precaution. You're moving everyone from the houses around mine, hoping that limits the people involved."

"Someone might get hurt anyway."

"Yes, that's true." She looked as if she drifted into a memory.

"I haven't forgotten your friends in Austin. And I haven't forgotten that your mother-in-law and her friend were assassinated. That's six people in your life who have already died."

"Just don't let the next one be you." She tapped him on the tip of his nose and smiled softly. "I don't know if I can handle that."

The debate he'd been having with himself turned into full-blown doubt. How could he have expected her to face their unknown opponent? She wasn't a professional. She hadn't even asked for his help.

Yet, here she was accepting his plan of action as the only choice she had. She moved to a chair and sipped at her coffee.

"I want you to know that it took all my willpower to let you get some rest this morning instead of making love to you again." He picked up his mug. "Pretty much still true."

"We'll have more time together after this is finished. Want some eggs or do we need to get on the road? Have you talked to Fred?"

"You believe that, right? You're not just saying we'll have more time because it sounds good?" He had a moment of panic that if all things didn't go well, she'd disappear again. She was already good at it and this time she had a town full of reasons.

"Don't you believe it?"

"Well, yeah. But I'm the kind of guy that knows what he wants and goes after it." And when all was said and done...he wanted her.

"So am I what you want, Ranger Johnson? Or am I an assignment you need to finish? Maybe you should think about that before you answer."

He didn't need to think. Realizing that she needed to wait, well, that was okay. He could handle that she needed time. A lot had happened in the past week.

A lot more would happen in the next couple of days.

"How do you like your eggs? I noticed you have some biscuits, too. Those are the two things I can make with confidence. Besides tea, lemonade and sangria." She pushed back from the table. "It's a solid plan. I'm glad you came up with it. And knowing Fred like I do, there's no telling what he would have done otherwise."

"I'll give Fred a call and make sure everything's set. Cook whatever you want. We're not in a rush."

"Famous last words." She gathered her items.

He retrieved his phone, but planned to call Fred on speaker so Kylie could hear. Fred would want to know she was all right. Biscuits were in the oven and she cracked eggs in the bowl. He walked in just in time to catch her fishing out a piece of eggshell.

"Don't laugh at me."

"Oh, I'm not. I'm a terrible cook. If you use a larger piece of the shell, you can scoop it out faster for some reason. Learned that after crunching my own eggs a couple of times."

She used half the eggshell and started whipping the eggs. "Good tip. Where did you learn that? In fact, I hardly know anything about you."

"You know all the important things."

"Right." She nodded her head with an all-knowing smile. "You don't care what your house looks like. You don't like sunscreen, burn and then tan. You have a pool you rarely use. You know how to chop wood. And you're pretty good in bed. Did I miss anything?"

He laughed with her.

"I have four nephews I like a lot. I was raised on a ranch about three hours west of here."

"Really? A ranch with horses and cows, those sorts of things?"

"Yes." He looked toward the eggs, trying to

get her attention without jumping up to mix them around the hot pan. She had a list of questions, genuinely excited about visiting a ranch. He lifted a finger pointing to the stove. It didn't work.

"Do your parents still live there?"

If the eggs she scrambled were a burned mess, he'd eat every bite. He admired her effort for trying. He remembered his mom's one or two tries at cooking. She and Kylie would have at least one thing to talk about. Now all he had to do was tell her she'd be meeting them that afternoon.

"I guess you'll find out soon enough," he answered.

Were they hiding their anxiety about luring the shooters into the open by talking about his family? Did he care as long as she remained relaxed and calm?

"Oh, you mean providing we survive this adventure and live to start the next." She finally scrambled the egg mixture in the pan.

"Well, sort of." He checked his text messages. His dad expected them around two and said that the ranch was guest free. "I think those biscuits might be done. Did you set a timer?"

"I didn't see one." She left the pan, pulling drawers open to find a pot holder.

"Want some help?"

"No. Go ahead and call Fred." She waved the oven mitt over the very dark brown biscuits.

"I think I'll wait till after breakfast." *And I'm sure the house hasn't burned to a crisp.*

"What are your parents like?"

He shrugged, wanting to jump up and pull the pan from the burner. "Normal, I guess." He stayed put because he'd never seen Kylie so relaxed.

"Am I being too nosy asking why you let your mother hire a decorator? Why would they want to spend all that money on something you don't really like?"

"Shoot, it's worse than that. She spent my money."

"I thought you said you worked for the Texas DPS Highway Patrol before joining the Rangers."

"I did." He slurped his coffee watching the real question form in her eyes. She wanted to know how he could afford it. "My family's business is, let's say, a successful one."

"Well, that's good. Hopefully you don't have to worry about it while you're working here."

No worries at all. She'd find out that money wasn't an issue when she met his parents that afternoon. It would be safer to hang out there, surrounded by all his dad's security. Bryce intended on taking her yesterday before he'd been distracted in the pool. And other things.

Something was different about her... It was right in front of him. He could see the skin on her arms. She wasn't wearing a long-sleeve shirt. His heart did a backflip. He couldn't make a big deal about it. He wanted to, but his instincts told him no.

He also wanted to destroy the person who had marred her with that scar. Wanted to put them away where they couldn't hurt or kill anyone again. His gut told him that was a strong possibility.

But not now. Today was meet-the-parents day and he didn't know if Kylie was ready for Cheryl and Blackhat Johnson.

Chapter Seventeen

Kylie loved the drive to the ranch. They hadn't been silent because of tension or arguing. Just the opposite. She'd spent most of the ride asking questions about her new phone. They listened to one of his songs and then she'd skip forward until she found one she liked. Bryce looked casual behind the wheel, but there was a layer of tension she assumed was because they had to be on guard.

When they arrived at the gate, the guard on duty recognized Bryce and waved him through. Kylie stiffened in her seat, finally feeling the tension obviously flowing from Bryce.

"This isn't a big deal, right?" she asked. "I mean…there's not going to be twenty questions or anything about how we met? No misunderstanding why I'm here?"

"I explained everything to my dad already and he said we could stay in the guesthouse. It might just be meals?" Bryce shrugged not really committing or answering her question.

They got out of the truck and he tangled their lips together in a deep kiss. It would have lasted longer, but they were interrupted by someone clearing his throat.

"Want me to come back later?"

"Dad!"

"That would be me. Who's this?"

Bryce turned back to her, bringing her close to his side. "Kylie Scott, this is my dad, Blackhat Johnson."

"Pleased to meet you and have you here at the Rockin' J. Cheryl is going to flip when she sees you. Come on to the main house."

"You did tell her that we want to stay in the guesthouse?"

"Sure thing. Why wouldn't I?" He shrugged shoulders just as broad as his son's. "Course, she's not standing for that. Main house or the barn. Yeah, I think that's what she said."

"Dad." Bryce stretched the word into three syllables like a kid.

A striking woman almost as tall as Kylie ran across the yard and threw herself into Bryce's arms. She kissed his check with a loud, artificial smack and then pushed him away. It took a few seconds for it to register that it must be Bryce's mother.

"You're such a bad kid to stay away from home like you do."

"Good to see you, too, Mom."

"You know I'm teasing. So this is Kylie? I'm Cheryl and we're so glad to have you visit. Are you sure we can't invite a couple of people over—"

"No one," Bryce interrupted and pulled Kylie back to his side.

Bryce had his arm around her as they passed through the side door. He was quickly tugged away from her by his dad and replaced by his mom. Cheryl escorted her inside and through a ginormous foyer.

"Are you guys tired? Want to retreat to a bedroom, hon? We have plenty of those." His mother ignored the shaking of Kylie's head and waved at a woman cleaning the stove. "Lorie G, sweetheart, can you please make up one of the rooms that opens to the patio? That will be nicer for Kylie in the morning. Do you swim, hon?"

"She just got here, Mom. Can't the interrogation wait a bit?"

"We're all so excited to meet a friend of our son's. And, Bryce Johnson, am I supposed to ignore our guest because she just arrived? How long has it been since you both ate? Johnson! Where is that man?"

"He's checking on extra security, Mom."

"There's more security out there than the

President's ranch. So food? Rest? Or just a big margarita?"

"Mom." Bryce sang her title like the kid who had said "Dad" earlier.

"Bryce, go help your father or go see what's in the fridge. Either way…you leave us alone for a while. It's been so long since I've gotten the scoop from anyone younger than me. Especially a woman."

Kylie loved Bryce's mom instantly. She was bubbly and so full of life moving through the simple ranch house—her inaccurate description of the twenty-odd-room house and studio.

Cheryl Johnson had memorabilia sitting around and loved talking about where each piece had come from. The house was one hall after another. The center of everything could be considered a great room with a huge fireplace in the middle. Bryce's mom encouraged Kylie to look around, asked if she enjoyed margaritas and went to the bar to make a pitcher.

Kylie didn't mention she didn't drink. The explanation would bring the conversation back to her own past. She was more curious about Bryce and his family.

"Is the dragon from China?" Kylie wasn't about to pick it up. She'd had a similar very expensive piece in her former life.

"Yes, Johnson brought that back from a tour when I was pregnant with the youngest. I normally traveled with him back then. That ivory carving of an elephant is something he picked up from the Japan tour for Bryce when he was three. At least I think that was the year."

Tour? It would be insulting to ask what kind of tour. That's something you should know before staying overnight with the parents. Right? She had no clue since Bryce hadn't mentioned it. Or anything other than that their business was successful.

Next to the dragon was a set of drumsticks and a picture encased in crystal. It looked as though it was Bryce's parents and…

"Isn't that Duff McKagan from Guns N' Roses?"

"Yes. Johnson was an emergency replacement for a Dallas concert. It was sweet of him to send us that as a thank-you." She stirred the ingredients.

"He tried to pick me up at a party once."

"I had to keep a close eye on our baby girl when she came to a concert. All four kids performed on stage at one time or another with Johnson, but when she got older, guys would hit on her, too." Cheryl shook her head, tsking under her breath. She poured salt onto a plate then began dipping the glass rims. "We've got all their pictures in the movie room. Go ahead and take a look. I'll bring these in a sec."

It was hard not to want to take a peek. After everything that had happened, Kylie was ready for some normalcy and alone time. If she retreated to her bedroom, she'd break down. She'd rather be curious about Bryce and his life before becoming a Texas Ranger.

The movie room had four sections of wall space dedicated to family pictures. Each featured a different child. Three were performance pics of Bryce's siblings from various ages to adulthood, some with celebrities, some on stage alone. But the ones she was most curious about had one picture with a famous singer and then…horses.

"He was barely five there and such a cutie. I think he wore his hair slicked back for a couple of weeks rehearsing for that show."

"Is that really Frankie Valli?"

"Oh, yes. Johnson has played with just about everybody. It's been a wild ride at times." Cheryl handed her the margarita, then pointed at the back of the stage in the picture. "See that miniature drum set? Bryce played those."

Kylie held the cold glass, but didn't have a real desire to take a sip. That was Sissy's thing and didn't really interest her any longer.

"It was just one song, Mom. And I was so bad, Dad never asked me to do it again." Bryce laughed and took the margarita from her hand, sipping before he pulled her close. "I like the rodeo pictures better."

"You just preferred horses," Blackhat said over his wife's shoulder. "You were never bad, son. Where did you get that idea?"

"There's much more to that story than either of

them is willing to tell." Cheryl looked back and forth between father and son. "Seriously, you don't remember, Bryce?"

"I remember it was an awful experience."

"Do you really not remember what happened that night?" his dad asked.

Bryce shook his head. His parents stared at each other.

When no one continued the conversation, she was torn about asking. Kylie was super curious. More than wondering what would happen to the Tenorenos. Not as much as imagining what might happen in her new relationship with Bryce. She could ask Bryce later, but he seemed genuinely in the dark so she wouldn't be able to find out later from him.

"I really don't know what they're talking about," Bryce answered.

"Do you mind if I ask what happened?" She looped her fingers around his upper arm and tugged him to stay put. Did she have the right? She didn't know. But she wanted it. Since he stayed, she hoped it was willingly because he didn't mind her knowing.

Cheryl looked at Blackhat and he shrugged. "Beats me why he doesn't remember. Maybe he's stared at his computer screen too long and it fried his memory circuits."

Cheryl playfully swatted him, then hugged his arm, weaving her fingers through his. "That oldies benefit was in Austin. Johnson was playing for several artists. Bryce performed and I was waiting at stage left for him. He exited stage right and before I could make my way around to that side, he'd disappeared. He was gone for about half an hour."

"You guys never talked about this." Bryce's muscles tensed under her palms. He looked at her, confused. "It's the first I'm ever hearing about going missing."

"It's why we bought this place," his dad laughed. "Don't you remember getting that badge Mom keeps on the kitchen bulletin board?"

"The toy star?"

"Honey…" Cheryl gave him an all-knowing look only a mother could. "That's the real thing given to you by the man who found you. After that you didn't want to have anything to do with the drums. Like your dad said, we bought this place. You learned how to ride and were focused on becoming a Texas Ranger."

"Where did he go? Did someone try to kidnap him?" Now Kylie wanted the entire story.

"He never told us. He was found several blocks away. Good thing you knew your name. The ranger knew the song you were singing and had a feeling you belonged to someone at the '60s benefit concert. Bryce made it back before the police could begin their search. That's why the papers and television never got the story."

"You've never sung since," his dad said.

"He sang for me," she admitted before thinking much about the importance. All three faces brought the significance to her attention.

"Was it 'Can't Take My Eyes Off You'?" Cheryl asked in a whisper.

"Yes."

"Cool," Cheryl and Blackhat said together. They looked at each other and hugged, shaking their heads. Then Cheryl let out a soft *squeee*.

"Don't read anything into that." Bryce dropped his chin to his chest.

Kylie tried. Really tried not to believe what his parents were implying. But it didn't work. She spent the rest of the night thinking of what could be right with Bryce instead of everything that had been wrong for so long.

KYLIE WAS LYING next to Bryce on the patio listening to music later that afternoon. His parents had left them alone just a few minutes before. She was drifting, letting the hot sun hypnotize her into deep oblivion. Someplace she didn't have to wonder about what would happen tomorrow.

"Still awake, Kylie?"

"If I have to be." She was completely content not to move or think.

"I don't think it's necessary for you to go to Hico and draw these guys into the open. Just bringing the car to the house should accomplish that. It's safer if you stay here with Dad's security. I spoke with my father earlier and he's cool with it."

She couldn't raise her voice to argue. She also couldn't make an argument for or against a plan that he hadn't told her about yet.

They'd been sitting in silence and she'd actually thought he'd fallen asleep. Kylie turned to her side, leaning on her elbow. She attempted to be calm even though her heart was racing ninety to nothing at his out-of-the-blue decision. "If the plan isn't safe enough for me, then call the whole thing off."

"It's still a good plan that could work."

"Then I need to be a part of it."

"But—"

"No buts. No exceptions. I have to do this. I thought you understood that." They hadn't explicitly said the words aloud. But she had thought he understood because she'd been included from the beginning.

"I get it. I just…"

"Last week at my house convinced me that no one is safe around me. Even if I start over in another town, maybe even in another state, I'd be putting people in danger. I have to face whoever tried to kill me five years ago, Bryce. No more running. No more people hurt because of me."

He took her hand in his and rolled to his back. "I had to try."

And so did she…only she needed to succeed.

Chapter Eighteen

The outside walls and windows had been repaired on her house—or Fred's house since he was the one that rented it to Kylie. The inside had been picked up, swept clean of glass and the destroyed items removed. The bedroom was okay and her laptop was safe inside that room.

After the drive, she excused herself and checked on her gun safe. The handgun was still in the bathroom. Either Bryce had forgotten about it, or he trusted that she at least wouldn't pull it on him.

"Officer Harris and Fred made certain everyone was off the street." Bryce told her when she joined him in the living room. "I'm surprised that everyone was so cooperative."

"Why here? Why couldn't we do this at Fred's place outside city limits?"

"We talked about it and agreed they'd think it was a trap."

"But not this? I mean, it's summer and there are no kids on the block. No one driving anywhere."

"We can't have everything."

"In the meantime, we're sitting ducks here. Will the walls hold up if they start firing that cannon at us again? Fred didn't have time to get another refrigerator." She hadn't been thrilled with the idea of trying to trap the men after her. Honestly, she'd agreed solely because she knew Bryce and Fred had already committed to it. The wheels had been put into motion without her.

"It'll be okay." Bryce wrapped his arms around her, hugging tight. "I've been wondering—only a little, mind you—about something."

"What are you wondering only a little about?" She tried to smile at his attempt to cheer her.

"How come there's no Mister Kylie?"

"If you're asking why I'm not married, I didn't want to become involved with anyone with this—" She drew a circle around her. "—situation hanging over my head. It wasn't fair to bring anyone else into the uncertain future I have."

"Had. We're remedying part of that problem today."

She wished. Hoped. Prayed it would be over. "How about you? Why aren't you married yet instead of just uncle of the year?"

"Haven't met that right person. My dad once looked at my mom and told me to fall in love completely. Not halfway. I can't tell you how many times he said not to expect the person you love to fill you fifty percent. 'It's all the way or not at all.' One hundred percent all of you...that's love."

"Those sound like song lyrics."

"Probably. My dad is a drummer, remember?" He shrugged. "I've never been that much in love with anyone. But I figured if it worked for my parents, maybe I should wait for the real thing."

Bryce's phone buzzed and they separated for him to look at the message.

"Fred just texted. He just got to town. He stopped at the Koffee Cup to buy pie."

"Nothing like setting priorities."

"Good move. We get pie and somebody might see the car since the shop is on the corner." Bryce rubbed his hands together in a greedy motion.

"You better tell him to get coffee, too. The coffeemaker was shot to pieces."

Bryce typed a text and looked up. "I'm going to open the garage so he can drive inside." He pointed to the folding chair and what lay on top of it. "Time to put that on."

"You're not wearing yours."

"I will be. The vest is the only way I can protect your heart." He left through the front, stopping on the porch to tap on his phone.

The bulletproof vest was heavy. Bryce had already adjusted it to fit her. She assumed one of the police officers had borrowed it for her since HICO PD was printed across the front and back.

It was only a few minutes until they had plastic forks in one hand and pie containers in the other. Bryce stood next to the front window, Fred at the back. She sat in a folding chair in the hallway.

"I can't believe I didn't know about this pie. I've driven through Hico a lot over the years to get to the ranch." Bryce put another mouthful of banana blueberry cream into his mouth, then another. He looked guilty. What had he said? Was he afraid Fred would frown on his background?

"Your parents never stopped either?" Fred asked.

"No, sir. They don't drive much."

"I thought you said they traveled a lot and you stayed home."

"I did. I mean, they did travel. Do. My dad's a pilot. They own a sweet Piper Cherokee that they take to major airports." He scraped the bottom of his container. "My dad's threatened to fly and get a gallon of milk before. The Rockin' J is a long way from everything."

"Wait a minute. Your parents own the Rockin' J?" Fred asked like everyone knew what that meant. "Blackhat J is your dad?"

"I knew he was a drummer and has played with some famous people." Kylie quirked an eyebrow in his direction. "They never implied that people would recognize his name."

"Kylie, Blackhat J has played with the best rock and roll bands in history. He's in the Rock and Roll Hall of Fame. You met him?"

"I stayed there the past couple of days."

"It's no big deal. He's just a drummer." Bryce supplied reluctantly, shrugging. "I'd be happy to change the subject now. And would appreciate it if you kept this info to yourself, Fred."

"If you insist." Fred looked a little sulky.

"So he and your mom traveled and you stayed at home?" She reminded him of one of the few things he'd said about his family. "You don't fly much?" Sarcastically adding.

"Not commercially. And I did stay home, traveling made me sick as a kid. When I was a teen, I had commitments at school. My siblings didn't feel the same way and traveled all over the place. But I knew what I wanted and the only way to get it was to stay in school, go to college."

It was the first time she'd seen Bryce flustered, embarrassed, talking too fast. He didn't seem to enjoy his parents' status and looked uncomfortable.

"How come the Rangers didn't play up who your daddy was? They make big deals of politicians and military grads all the time." Fred finished his pie and took a long gulp of his coffee.

"I didn't tell them." Bryce's pie was set to the side as he looked through the blinds. "Changing the subject, we're sure all the houses were cleared?"

"Yes. Harris and I checked in with everyone."

"Even the house on the corner that normally has the big rig out back?"

"That would be Grant Fenley's place. No one was home early this morning. His wife has a sister in Meridian. Want me to have somebody follow up?"

"It may be a ceiling fan or something, but the curtain keeps fluttering."

"I can have Harris check it out again—"

"Let's wait." Bryce interrupted and stared out the window. "Something just doesn't feel right."

"You guys told me the plan for getting here. So what happens now?" She was curious, of course. But were they really just going to wait around for an attack? "What do you think those men plan to do?"

"We thought they'd…well…try to get you." Fred scratched his stubble whiskers.

"Even after my confrontation with Xander in Austin?"

Fred plopped all four legs of his chair back to the floor. "What's this? You talked to Tenoreno?"

"He wanted me to sign annulment papers. I got away before he could do anything threatening. You don't need to get upset, Fred." Kylie stood in the hallway, able to see both men, feeling the weight of the situation as well as the bulletproof vest on her shoulders. "Oh, and he acted like he hadn't known I had the car all this time."

"So he didn't think you had the Cadillac? You know, Bryce, that's always bothered me. From the time Kylie drove that classic convertible into town I expected to find a stolen vehicle report on it. That's why I was so fast to believe Kylie was the intended target."

"If they aren't looking for Kylie, then what are they...?" Bryce nodded his head "The car? They actually want the Cadillac. What's inside it? I'm assuming you checked it out?"

"Didn't let her park it here until I did. But there's nothing. Trunk is clear. I searched for blood, debris, drugs. No papers, nothing in the glove box except a bottle of whiskey that I gave to Kylie."

"I didn't know you did all that, Fred."

"Darlin', we might have wanted to play the Good Samaritans when you arrived, but I couldn't have lived with myself if I let you bring drugs into town. I hung up my badge, but not my good sense."

"Why wouldn't Tenoreno report it stolen? If he was after Kylie it would have been the fastest way to find her." Bryce rubbed his forehead as if he was tired of thinking about all the possible whys.

"Unless, he really didn't know I had the car. He said as much in Austin." She'd been trying to piece it together in her mind throughout the morning. "There's one thing Xander didn't mention. The shooting. He didn't smirk or brag or anything like that. Which actually says more. He's the kind of guy who would have pointed out how unsafe it is without him around."

"If the police had picked you up with a stolen vehicle, they could have searched it. So something has to be inside."

"There's nothing in that car," Fred said with more conviction.

"Nothing obvious." Bryce left his window. "Can you get Richard to watch the Fenley house more closely? Kylie, come with me. Fred? Key?"

"There ain't nothing in that car," Fred mumbled, tossing the key. "I'll tell Richard."

Kylie followed Bryce into the garage. He slipped the Cadillac key back onto the ring she'd grabbed from the Tenoreno rack so many years ago.

"What do you hope to find?"

When she got near, he stole a lingering kiss. "I've been wanting that ever since Fred arrived. And have I told you how sexy you look in that vest?"

"Why are you buttering me up, Ranger Johnson?" Kylie smiled at him. Who wouldn't want that smoldering kiss? "Is it because now that we've *slept* together you think you can ask me to hide and I will?"

"I didn't say a word." He held up his hands as if he was defenseless.

"You're thinking it. Open the trunk and start looking." She raised her voice to be heard inside,

"I think you're a very thorough man, Fred. I bet you looked under the seats."

"Yes, ma'am. I think I spent the quarter I found."

"So there's no reason for me to look there." She took a flashlight off the shelf. "I'll slide under the car and see if anything's noticeable."

"I'll do that." He lifted the flashlight from her hand. "You take the trunk so you don't have to take off the vest."

Bryce was under the car before she could think of a response. There was nothing inside the black carpeted area. The ridges were still there from being vacuumed.

She stared into the darkness. It was one of those moments where she really couldn't think of what to do next. Fred had searched the car but she agreed that Xander's interest in the car was unusual. Something had to be here.

"A car doesn't seem like a very safe place to hide something important enough to kill over. It would have to be secure and other than taking the car completely apart, how would we find it? Xander could have bought a safe or rented a safety deposit box. His father had a safe. Why use an old car he rarely drove?"

"We don't have time to unscrew every screw. And I would imagine he wanted to keep it away from everybody or this was a temporary place."

"Except the other person shooting at us. Don't

you see? At least two people knew something was hidden. The man shooting at us last week seemed to know about the car, too."

Bryce scooted his head from under the back. "You're right."

"Are you through with the flashlight?" She took it from his extended arm. As soon as he was free from the undercarriage, she crawled in the trunk. "I don't think Fred did this."

She lay on her back and aimed the beam of light into all the nooks and crannies of the car. The light reflected off something shiny stuck way back in the corner toward the seat. She used her feet to push herself closer and found a small lock.

"The key ring that you have, Bryce. Does it have a small one on it like for a lockbox?"

He put them in her hand, fingers around the smallest. She slipped the key into place and turned.

"A safe made for a car?" Fred asked from the doorway.

"Looks like it. Anything inside?" Bryce asked.

"Just this magnetic hide-a-key thingy." She handed it and the flashlight to Bryce. "Wait for me."

Once out of the car, they all stared at the tiny box as Bryce slid the top off. "A flash drive."

"I wonder what's on it?"

"Something to kill for."

"Okay, let's get the hell out of here." Fred whooped on his way up the step.

"Leave? Don't you want to catch those men? You've gone to so much trouble." Kylie dropped the key ring in her jeans pocket hoping they wouldn't listen to her. It was the one time she was playing devil's advocate and not wanting to be right.

"We have what they're after. We leave. Take this drive to Company F and find out what's on it in Waco. There's no reason to hang around here and risk our necks." Bryce stuck the drive in his jeans pocket.

"Fred?" The radio hanging on her friend's belt squawked. "Grant Fenley just drove up to his house. He has his kids with him."

Richard had been watching the street.

"Dammit," the older man said through gritted teeth. "Who let them through? Shoot, it doesn't matter. We'll come up with a plan B."

"It's okay, right?" she asked.

"Get in the car." A confused, worried look overtook Fred's face as he pointed to the convertible.

"No. I can shoot. For gosh sakes, Fred, you taught me how."

Bryce shrugged.

"Sorry, darlin'." Fred took that shrug as Bryce's agreement. "The car's the safest place for you."

"Oh, don't you 'darlin'' me with that sweet cowboy drawl." She tried to march past Bryce but

Fred blocked her and shut the door in her face. She heard the dead bolt turn. "I cannot believe you just locked me out of my own house!"

The garage was locked on the outside. No window. At least the light was on. She had the new cell that Bryce had purchased. Those guys weren't going to answer and they weren't going to change their minds. She was definitely stuck.

Chapter Nineteen

"You think she's safe in there?" Bryce asked the retired ranger and received a nod.

The radio walkie-talkie Fred held squawked again. "You want me to stay here or do something? Reckon those curtains are moving because someone's looking through them?" Richard surmised from Bryce's house.

"Tell him to stay put. I'll check it out."

"You guys have to let me out of here!" The shout was faint through the door.

"Forgive us, Kylie. We'll be right back." Fred turned to him. "I guess we should have, like, a knock or something so she'll know it's us."

"Or we could just call out to her. She'll probably recognize our voices."

"Kylie, we'll tell you it's us. If someone opens that door before we get back…find a shovel or something." Fred tapped on the door, indicating his departure. Then the older man turned to

Bryce. "I'll keep watch in the backyard while you check things out. No one will get inside here."

If there was a shovel in the garage, Kylie would probably take it to both of their heads when they got back. Bryce motioned for Fred to go out the back door.

"Just in case it's not a fan blowing those curtains, you take the long way and approach Fenley's house from the north. I'll give you a couple of minutes since you have the longer ground to cover." He tapped the radio. "We work together."

"Got it. Put on the vest, son."

"Heading for it now, sir." Bryce had a moment... just a moment where he wanted to say something poignant, but he couldn't think of a thing. They nodded at each other and split. "No matter what happens, keep Richard inside. I'll give Harris a call and tell him the trouble we were expecting may have showed up."

Fred darted to Kylie's big tree in the back, then through the back gate of the privacy fence. He must have removed the locks earlier since there was no pause in the stealth of his journey.

But locking Kylie inside wasn't a great idea. He just didn't have time to explain himself. Bryce did an about-face and unlocked the garage door. Kylie jumped up from the step, dipped her head and marched into the kitchen.

"It's a good thing you came back here, bust—"

Bryce pulled her body to his, capturing her lips

and shushing her lecture. "I didn't want to argue with you or Fred. The door is ready for you to open if you need to get out of here fast. Wait." He covered her tender lips with his finger. "*If* things go wrong. Drive straight to the police station. Don't try to outrun them to anywhere else. Got it?"

"This is my fight, I don't want to run."

"Promise me. I need to know you'll be safe."

"I promise. Don't get shot or worse. We have whatever they're looking for now. We can—"

"First we have to get the Fenley family out of there." He saw the panicked look in her eyes, heard the sudden intake of breath as if she was about to make a speech. "I know what you're about to say. That this is your problem and no one else is supposed to get hurt. I want to be clear. Exchanging yourself for them won't help. So don't think about it."

"So you want me to stay here and twiddle my thumbs?"

"Yes. And stay alert listening to the radio. We need you to talk to Hico PD, keep them up-to-date on what's happening. I got to get going."

"Bryce." She sandwiched his face between her palms and kissed him. "Don't be long. We have things to do."

"Yes, we do. Go grab that handgun from behind your picture in the bathroom." He winked at her split-second of astonishment before heading to the front door.

Staying close to the house, he searched the vicinity for guns pointed his direction. He wanted to check out the Fenley house and find everything perfectly normal. They'd evacuate the family and everything would be back on track. But his gut told him this was it. Tenoreno's men had been waiting on them instead of the other way around. He pulled the bolt on the garage so the door could be raised from the inside.

Taking off down the driveway, he pulled the Velcro tight at his ribs and drew his Sig, wishing it was a shotgun. He was better with a shotgun. Easier to hit his target. In this case, the better scenario would be that he wouldn't have a target at all.

Walking in the street, he passed the rooster and hen belonging to Kylie's neighbor. A cat watched them from the bottom limb of a mimosa tree. How the chickens were still alive...no idea.

"Hey, Todd." He kept the phone on speaker. "Things might get hairy around here in a minute."

"I'm at the end of Pecan by the statue."

The Fenley family had two kids, eleven and eight. The rig that Grant drove was out back where it had been absent that morning. A two-foot cement wall outlined the property. A small pink bicycle was safely parked by the front steps.

Porch swing, chairs, small table, birdhouses,

plants and a cow-shaped message chalkboard all worked together to make the place look lived-in. The house itself was long and not too wide. The curtain dropped, covering whoever was behind it.

It wasn't a ceiling fan.

Three or four more steps and he could dive next to that rock wall. He heard the crack of a glass pane and he hit the ground. The street was peppered with bullets just behind him.

The small pieces popped up hitting him in the back, pinning him with his face in the dirt. Small glass-like rocks dug into the back of his left hand. His right still held his Sig close to his chest. When a pause came in the shots, he retrieved his phone and called Todd Harris.

"Shots fired out west window. I'm pinned at the street. Fred's coming from the north, can you approach from the east?"

"Got ya covered."

Bryce was about to signal Fred on the radio, but the shots began in earnest again and stopped just as suddenly. He readied his Sig and risked a look over the wall. The porch screen door was kicked open, bursting the spring and slamming shut. He watched a booted foot toe the door open.

A thirty-something man was pushed forward, stumbling onto the porch, immediately getting to his knees. "Don't shoot! You can't shoot! Please don't shoot!"

"Drop to the ground, Grant," Todd called out.

Bryce couldn't see where the officer was from his position at the wall.

"I can't," the guy on the porch said. "I have to stay here or they'll…they'll kill my kids."

"You okay, Bryce?" Fred asked on the radio. "The shades are drawn. I have no target from my position."

"I have eyes on the porch, but I'm blind for the rest of the house."

"Johnson? Bryce Johnson?" Grant called.

"I'm here."

"They said all they want is a woman named Sissy and a car." Grant turned a bloodied ear toward the door. "I mean the Cadillac. It has to be a Cadillac. Then they'll let my kids go."

"Bryce," Kylie broke in on the radio.

"Out of the question," he shouted, wanting to stand to let them know who was in charge. But his instincts kept him beside that wall.

Behind him he heard the garage door go up. "Kylie, no!" Half into the radio and half down the street, he roared to get her to listen to him. He caught himself. Screaming wouldn't work, he had to reason with this woman he'd come to care about so much.

"We can't trust them, Kylie," Fred said.

"Trust me," he pleaded into the radio.

It was too late. The car was rumbling on the street and she wasn't responding to the radio pleas.

She drove slowly. He could have easily run alongside if he'd been across the street.

He rose, ready to move. Shots from the house hit the street just behind him.

"Don't do it, Johnson! God, I'm begging you please. They've got a gun to my son's head." Grant was weeping.

Kylie rolled the window down. "It's my turn to fix the problem, Bryce. I can't let those kids get hurt."

"Johnson," Grant called for his attention. "They want you to throw down your guns. Kylie's supposed to drive. What?" He turned back to the door and reached into the dark room.

Grant Fenley's hands were zip-tied together as he walked down the porch and sidewalk. "Sorry, Kylie. I need to lock you to the steering wheel."

"I'll be okay, Grant. Don't worry about it." She placed her hands on the wheel again and Grant did as he was instructed then returned to the house.

"I can't just let you drive to your death." Bryce was close enough he didn't have to raise his voice.

"I'm not. I'll meet you in Austin." Her eyes looked toward his pocket. "You still have bargaining power."

He couldn't answer before two masked men— backs together—moved from the house. One carried the little girl. One held a gun to the eleven-year-old's head. Grant wasn't near them.

Both of the kids were blindfolded. Bryce couldn't let this happen. He got to his feet, resting his Sig on the wall and raising his hands in the air.

"We don't want any trouble, Ranger," the one holding the girl said, spinning a little away from his partner.

"Take me instead of the kids."

"No offense," the other man said, "but you won't keep your partners from shooting at us. These guys will."

Bryce didn't move. He didn't even shake his head or look anywhere except into the cocky one's eyes. "Come on, man. Where do you think you can drive this car and not be seen? The State Troopers will have you in their sights or a helicopter will be on your tail by the time you pass the city limits. Why don't you hand over your guns without anybody getting hurt? You tell us who hired you and why, and I'm sure we can make a deal."

"Stay back, Ranger."

"I'm back, I'm back," Bryce answered as calmly as his racing pulse could manage. "But if you take the kids, there's nothing I can help you with. You catch my meaning?"

The men's backs were a little farther apart now, inching their way down the sidewalk. Bryce wanted to rush them himself. He'd have to step up on the two-foot wall and hit the ground running again. He was too far away to use the border wall to his advantage and launch himself from it.

No, he didn't have options. Hands in the air, gun on the rocks, girl cuffed in the car, kids with barrels to their temples. He'd lost.

Or definitely lost control of the situation.

The gunmen were almost at the car and didn't look like they had any intention of releasing the kids. Fred and Todd were within sight. The other police officer sirens were close. He was out of ideas. The situation was about to turn from worst possible scenario to completely—

"You can take me to Xander, but those kids are staying here," Kylie commanded, revving the engine on the Cadillac. "I'm serious. And the only ride you've got."

"Kylie—"

"No one else gets hurt because of me! Does everyone hear that?" she yelled.

"You don't call the shots, bitch. We're in charge."

Bryce closely observed the body movements of the men. One had a looser grip on the boy, but the other shifted the girl and held her tighter.

They weren't letting her go.

Everything happened in seconds…

Two police cars blocked the street running north and south. The mouthy one shoved the boy to the ground. The gunmen both broke into a run, the girl squirming and crying. Bryce scooped up his Sig and aimed. The men ran around the trunk.

The boy was yelling for his father. Grant was screaming from the doorway. The gunmen were fast enough and smart enough to turn in circles, keeping the girl between them and most of the cops.

Multiple gun barrels pointed at the Cadillac.

No one had a shot.

If anyone fired…people would die.

"Hold your fire!" Bryce shouted, pointing his Sig to the clouds. "Hold your fire!"

"Smart choice, Ranger man!" one of them shouted as he jerked open the door and shoved his partner and the girl inside.

Bryce could only stare as they forced the little girl to crawl in the wide back window and both men sank low into the seats. He connected with Kylie as she sadly looked his way, but gunned the engine.

Tires spun on the edge of the road. No vehicles would block their exit past the Billy the Kid statue at the end of the street.

Bryce ran after them. There was no shot to take. They couldn't shoot the tires. If the car rolled the little girl would be killed. If they shot at the men, they could easily kill the girl or Kylie.

"You had to let them go, son. No choice." Fred said, looping an arm across Bryce's shoulders.

Where had this all gone so wrong?

He turned to Todd. "Get on the phone. Company F, police, troopers, statewide bulletin, everything. Do your job and find that car!"

Bryce ran up the street to his truck.

The radio squawked, "They turned east toward Meridian."

Squawked again, "Don't let them see you following!"

Richard and a couple of others stood in the front yards with shotguns and rifles on their hips. They'd tried. They'd all tried. But this was on him. His mistake. He'd let Kylie and the Fenley girl down.

"They really took Darla, too?" Richard asked.

Bryce didn't have time to acknowledge him. He started the pickup, tore out of the driveway and down the street after Kylie. He pressed his contacts for Major Parker. No answer.

Cursing, he banged the steering wheel with the edge of his fist. He was three minutes behind them. He pushed the truck to the max. Six miles out of town. Seven. Eight. Still no sign of them.

"Where the hell did they go?"

Chapter Twenty

The men had used plain zip ties to lock Kylie's wrists to the center of the steering wheel. She could barely turn a corner, but managed. Minutes past the city limits sign, the masked man next to her grabbed the wheel and yanked hard to the right. She thought her arms had cracked as she fell sideways.

Sitting a quarter of a mile away, hidden from the road, was a semi-trailer truck and trailer. That's how they planned on getting away from the police who would be looking for the Cadillac.

"Hand me your phone," the man next to her commanded. "Line up with the ramps."

"I can't turn." He sliced through one of the plastic ties with a pocketknife and got out. She took the phone from her pocket, then lined the car up and was about to kill the engine when he reached through the window and pulled the switch for the top.

While the electric top folded into place between the trunk and backseat, he removed the phone's battery and threw the pieces into the brush. Her hope of Bryce following her with that bit of technology was tossed like the phone. She'd have to be more inventive. But she would get them free.

"Darla, honey. Climb over the seat to sit next to me."

She cooed to the crying girl, trying to calm her until the men had the top secured and motioned for her to pull onto the ramps. Once inside, a man who'd been waiting in the trailer squeezed along the edge of the car with more zip ties and a roll of duct tape.

Remembering some of the defensive research she'd allowed herself over the years, she flexed her wrists, making them as wide as possible. This man seemed to be younger and didn't realize her little trick would allow her to squeeze free.

Hopefully.

He tore a strip of tape to cover Darla's mouth.

"Please don't. She won't be able to breathe. We won't scream. Right, Darla? Promise him, sweetheart."

"Don't matter. I got orders," he said, reaching toward Darla who shoved herself to the far side of the vinyl seat. Her screams were those of a young child being yanked from her father and used as a human shield.

Kylie wanted to scoop the girl to her side and

protect her, comfort her. But her hands were secured. The man pushed Kylie forward into the steering wheel, leaning across her back to reach Darla. The little girl screamed more and at a higher pitch.

"Tell her to shut up!" he yelled.

"Please. Can't you see how scared she is?"

Kylie needed Darla free. Just in case she couldn't slip out of the zip ties, she needed the little girl to help. She saw the hesitation in the younger man's hands. He raised them, then dropped them again.

"Tell her to come over here and I'll do it real loose so she can get it off easy and breathe."

"Darla, did you hear? We can play a game, okay? He's going to put tape over our mouths and then we'll see if you can get yours off first. Okay? Can you do that?"

Darla nodded, looking terrified. But she got to her knees and hesitantly scooted closer. When she locked her hands around Kylie's upper arm, the guy looked somewhat less threatening as he placed the tape first on Darla and then on her. Now, if they'd leave them alone in the trailer…

The two men who had kidnapped Darla came on either side of the car. They yanked on her hands, testing them, and pulled the tie closer to her skin.

If her mouth hadn't been taped shut, she would have cursed like a sailor.

"Tape the kid's hands."

"She's just a kid. What's she going to do?" the younger one still holding the roll asked.

"Don't backtalk me, boy. Just do what I say."

"Yes, sir."

The one giving orders left the truck. Kylie watched him in the rearview mirror. He closed the first half of the double doors shut, bolting it into place. It was the first time in a very long time that hearing a secured lock didn't give her a feeling of elation and comfort.

"You ready, boy?" He began swinging the second door and the light inside their giant box began shrinking.

Darla's body shook next to her. The one referred to as "boy" jumped into the backseat and flipped on an electric camping lantern.

"Got it, sir."

The doors shut.

"If you move, I'll tape your hands and make you sit with me. Got it?"

Darla nodded her head, whimpering beneath the tape.

Kylie couldn't make her feel secure or at ease. All she could really do was breathe deeply through her nose to try to calm the racing of her own heart. Eight years old or not, Darla had a grip. Her fingernails were cutting into her flesh. Kylie hummed.

The lullaby "Mockingbird" immediately popped

into her head, more from seeing it in movies than personally hearing it. She hummed, saying the words in her head. There was no way she could slide her hands through the smaller loops around her wrists. Getting free now would involve Darla.

The kid bounced the car a bit as he stretched out. She heard the heels from his work boots hit the side of the car. The big rig lurched forward. She heard a click and they were plunged into darkness. Darla screamed behind the tape.

The one great thing about the horrific afternoon heat was that the inside of the big rig immediately began sweltering. Normally this wouldn't be a good thing. But today it made her upper lip sweat. And sweat helped loosen the tape across her mouth.

Boy, as the guy in charge referred to him, would soon be snoring. The rocking of rig, heat and darkness made it a perfect place to nap. But not relax if you were a captive, headed to a Mafia family to be killed.

Using her shoulder, she rubbed the corner of the tape, peeling it back slowly. Not waiting for it to dislodge from both sides, she lowered her voice, "Sweetie, can you pull the tape off now? It might sting a little. Be brave, little one, and don't cry. Can you do that?"

Kylie had to trust that the little girl was doing as instructed. No light seeped into their traveling box at all. The pitch-black made everything more frightening.

"I ain't asleep so stop trying to put one over on me." Boy clicked on a small penlight. "You both need to chill. We're gonna be here awhile."

Kylie saw Darla blink, then rub her eyes, between her own rapid adjusting. She couldn't see Boy's face, but one arm was relaxed across his belly. The other up and out of her view in the mirror. He was still stretched from window to window.

At least they weren't in the dark any longer. He'd said they were going to be there awhile. Did that mean Austin or somewhere no one would find them? The truck had been moving slowly and now seemed to be picking up speed.

There were three distinct noises she could hear—the truck, the almost panicked breathing from Darla and the deeper relaxed breathing from the backseat. She leaned forward and pulled the remaining tape from her skin.

It wasn't hard to catch Darla's gaze, she'd latched on to her again as soon as the light had come on. "Shh," she whispered. Kylie used her head to indicate for Darla to come closer.

"Sweetie, I need your help. You've got to be very careful and quiet as a mouse."

"Okay," she whispered as well as an eight-year-old could.

"See that shiny button over there? I need you to get me the knife that's inside."

Darla immediately shook her head.

"I know you aren't supposed to play with them, but this isn't playing. We need to hurry before he wakes up."

Darla hesitated and crawled to the glove compartment. Kylie pulled the steering wheel to the right, trying to turn the wheels and getting there inch by painful inch. Talking the little girl through how to release a zip tie...where was she going to get the descriptive words?

She wished there was a screwdriver, but she hadn't grabbed one from the garage. Just the very sharp utility knife Darla now had in her hand.

Chapter Twenty-One

"What about the cameras we set up on Main Street? They've got to show some traffic. We obviously didn't stop all the vehicles in and out of town. Grant got through." Todd gave instructions over the radio to the other Hico PD.

Bryce was alone in his truck, waiting at the apex of downtown Hico, listening to the radio chatter. All he needed was a direction and he was hightailing it after the Cadillac.

"When Grant got to the road block we instructed him to stay out of town. He agreed to head to his in-laws' place."

"Where is he? Has anybody had eyes on Grant Fenley? I want to talk with him." Fred interrupted inserting his own agenda.

"We're losing time," Bryce broke into the conversation. "Every minute that ticks by is another mile she's away from me. Gone. Got that? Now

give me something. Have the additional road-
blocks been set up?"

"Nothing's come through Meridian. Over."

He'd missed them. Trying to catch up with the
Cadillac, he'd missed that they'd detoured. "They
must have pulled off someplace, changed vehicles
and come back through town. Todd, have you got
that camera footage yet?"

"We let five cars past all with families. One
semi rig no markings headed northwest. One semi
transporting milk headed northwest. And Grant's
red tractor and trailer heading south toward his
family's place. Over."

"Somebody better find Grant Fenley. Something's fishy, Bryce. That red tractor couldn't be
his. I'm looking at the rig he parked at his house."
Fred's curse words broke off. "I think we need to
switch to cells. Somebody's probably monitoring
police frequencies."

Dammit. His phone buzzed on the seat next
to him.

"You think Fenley's in on this?" he asked Fred.

"Yeah. Do you have enough resources to com-
mit to the roads northwest and south?" Fred's
voice shook.

"It'll take time to get additional men and road-
blocks. And that's what they're counting on. So
they're probably closer than we think." Then why
did he feel like everything was lost?

"That's my guess, too." The older man sounded

resigned as if the same lost thoughts had crossed his mind. "Wherever they take her it'll have plenty of cover, might even be a building."

"A building will be more secure. They could switch rigs that way. Got anyplace around here that fits those parameters?"

"There's a couple of private airstrips in the area if they're planning to take Kylie out by plane."

"Fred, they don't need one. Just a field to land a helicopter and a building to hide the truck from the air."

"True."

Based totally on his gut, Bryce took off to the northwest. "Find Fenley. He's got to be involved, especially if we can track a rig just like his heading south."

"You think that's where they've taken our girls?"

"I can't know for sure, but I'm heading northwest. You head south following Fenley."

"Then you think it's a decoy." Fred sounded reluctant to chase down the least possible route.

Meaning the older ranger thinks they're heading this direction.

"Yeah. Be sure to take Richard with you. I'll call Todd and have him pin down where Fenley's wife could have gone."

The call to Officer Todd Harris was short and to the point. He was already solving the problem of the missing family. If Fenley had cooked up a deal with the kidnappers it didn't include his mother-in-law or his wife, who had her laptop tracing Grant's phone.

The family used a program showing where they were so the kids could find their dad on a map when he traveled across the country. Harris texted the coordinates. Bryce punched Find and never slowed down. Fenley's phone was fifteen minutes ahead in Dublin.

"Fred," he called. "Did you get Todd's text?"

"We've already turned around, but we're probably twenty-five behind you."

"I'll let you know what to expect. If not…"

"None of that, son. Everybody's coming out of this safe and sound. No exceptions."

Dublin PD were notified to watch the area but hang back until Bryce arrived. The call to Major Parker went as expected. The Rangers had been called in as soon as the Fenley girl was kidnapped. Rangers were on their way from different companies. All headed to Dublin, but none of them would get there sooner than him.

The sun shone through the windshield. It was a cloudless, deep blue sky. It would have been beautiful if he hadn't been racing to save the woman he loved. He hated having time to think about what they might be doing to her.

He had time for one more phone call. His stereo flashed Dialing. There was a gravelly hello through the speakers.

"Dad? I need a huge favor."

KYLIE WHISPERED INSTRUCTIONS to Darla, guiding her through sticking the tip of the utility knife in the release square—or whatever it was called—of the zip ties. It wasn't easy. In fact it was as scary as trying to remain undetected while they got it done.

The man guarding them remained asleep, but he could have jerked awake with any of the bumps from the truck. Maybe he'd been awake all night or something. It would explain why he never moved when the knifepoint stuck the back of her wrist and Darla gasped an "I'm sorry."

With one wrist free, Kylie could work the second one herself. The truck was slowing. Was it just for another small town or would they be opening those doors?

Hands free, she moved Darla into the passenger floorboard. "Stay quiet and as small as possible. No matter what happens. Promise?"

"Promise. Sorry I cut you."

"You did great," she whispered, then flipped over, scooted to stretch out until she could search under the driver's seat for the extra key. The tiny thing had stayed wedged where the seat was bolted to the floor. She slipped the key into the change pocket of her Wranglers, then thought better of it.

If someone searched her…she stuck the key back in its secure spot.

It was a long shot, but might get them both out of this mess…or at least be used for bargaining Darla's freedom. But first, she couldn't just wait to talk with Xander or even risk that begging for her life would satisfy him. Even waiting for a Texas Ranger wasn't the smart thing. She had to try to rescue herself.

She drew a deep breath, sitting behind the wheel. Boy had his gun wrapped between his arms and his chest. He was moving like someone about to wake. And the truck was slowing, turning, slowing more.

They'd arrived.

Kylie moved. Climbed. Planted her backside on the top of the front seat with one leg stretched across to the back. She balanced. Breathed. Prepared. She remembered the words of her instructor. Didn't let the importance of what she was attempting freak her out.

And most important, she remembered Bryce's caring touch that calmed her. His confidence made her whole. She had to do this for Darla, for Bryce…for herself.

The truck inched to a stop.

At the same moment she placed her boot heel on the man's throat, she plucked the handgun from his chest. Darla screamed. Boy startled awake, his hands going to her leg. She pulled the trigger over her head. The noise blasted her eardrums and the kickback of the weapon almost toppled her. She regained her balance by throwing both arms toward her captive.

"Let go of me." She removed her foot and straddled the seatback.

The doors opened with at least three guns aimed at her.

"Get up and get behind the wheel," she told Boy. If she could get out of the truck and the parking lot, she'd push this guy from the car and just keep driving until she found the police. "Start the car."

A slow clapping—just one person—started off to the side and joined the men at the back of the truck. All the men deferred to him. He was definitely in charge. And he was definitely *not* Xander.

"Very commendable, Sissy. Or should I call you Kylie now?"

Well-dressed, but in casual cool for Texas heat. He stood shorter than the rest of the men, so that meant shorter than her. He obviously knew who she was, but she didn't recognize him. It fit Bryce's theory that someone unknown to them wanted the car and her.

"Better think twice about your next move, Kylie," he said, hands on his hips. "I already have what I want." He waved his hand toward the Cadillac.

"Let the girl go and I'll do whatever you want." She barely glanced at Darla in the floorboard. "I'll let your man go as soon as I'm around a corner."

This lunatic would never let her drive away.

"You're mistaken, thinking I care about either of them. Again…" He waved a finger and the guns were aligned with her heart once more. "I already have what I want. You're only a bit of insurance."

He stepped from the area that she could see and spoke in a low grumble. Two additional men pulled the ramps over to a loading dock. Even if she could get the car out of the semi, she'd be stuck inside some sort of warehouse.

"What could you possibly want? There's nothing in this car. We've looked."

"Did you know that I restored this beauty? I lost her in a spur of the moment bet with your husband. The kind where I drove up in the Caddy and was left on a street corner before I could remove my belongings."

"Please just let us go. We have nothing to do with this."

"Bring him."

Bryce? Her heart dropped. Had he followed them as they left Hico and been caught trying to rescue her? His face was backlit by a warehouse light. She couldn't tell. The clothes were wrong. Tennis shoes, not boots. Bryce was still out there.

There was still hope if her ploy didn't work.

"I'm sorry, Kylie. They took my family," Grant Fenley said.

She might not be able to see his face, but she could see the gun pointed at his head. Without being told she dropped the weapon outside the car and watched it bounce underneath. Boy hopped over the door and she sank onto the seat, extending her arms for Darla to crawl to her lap.

"Don't get the idea that you bargained with me, Sissy," whatever his name was said. "If Xander had treated you the way I suggested, putting you in your place a couple of times, he would never have had you as a problem."

What?

This egotistical bastard thought he could have told Xander how to put her in her place five years ago. So he had been a part of her life back then. More importantly, he knew what was locked in that hidden safe.

What would happen if he realized the flash drive in the safe wasn't the right one? How was she going to protect Darla then?

Chapter Twenty-Two

"Kylie isn't heading to Austin. It's not Xander threatening her, although his involvement can't be completely ruled out." Bryce parked the truck as far as he could from the deserted grocery store where the Cadillac had been taken. "Fenley is a hostage. There must have been a third gunman in the house who forced him to drive the rig they put the car into."

"Wait on us, Bryce," Fred said over Richard stating something similar. "Don't rush in there on your own."

Kylie's ex-husband's path had crossed many times with the man giving the orders on that loading dock. Bryce knew everyone involved in the Tenoreno family dealings. Crime boss Daniel Rosco was considered a family friend.

Both the only sons of the Texas Mafia. Raised to be cruel and ruthless. He'd seen the file of accusations that should have had this man in prison a decade ago. Rosco's father had been brutally murdered by an assassin most likely hired by Xander Tenoreno.

So was this a revenge killing on the ex-wife? Or was something on the flash drive currently in his front pocket?

"I don't have eyes on Kylie or the girl yet. I need to get closer to see what's going on." And find out if Kylie was okay. He'd heard her name yelled by Fenley, but couldn't see past the semitrailer.

"Bryce—"

He disconnected. There wasn't any choice. He was the only person who could identify the kidnapped girl and Kylie. The Dublin police weren't equipped to deal with a hostage situation.

Hell, he wasn't either. There was just no choice.

Reversing the truck, he parked in front of the Dublin cop who became his shadow as soon as he'd hit town. Bryce could swear the young kid barely looked old enough to drive. The local PD had spotted the truck, notified him and retrieved a key to the building from the owner.

Bryce verified his phone was on Silent and grabbed his weapons. He handed the flash drive to Officer Trent Dawson, who knew enough of the story to copy the files onto his laptop. Bryce was most concerned about the kid opening them and becoming more involved. It was a risk he had to take. The state needed to see whatever was there, but Bryce needed the drive on his person for leverage.

Trent returned the drive and Bryce issued instructions that would be passed along to the other locals. They'd also be relayed to Fred and anyone else who showed up to help. Then he took off for the opposite side of the storefront, used the key to enter and began to snake his way through the empty aisles, reaching the back hallways to the warehouse.

"You would rather I hurt this beautiful little girl and her father? Come on, Sissy. Just hand over the key."

"The keys I had to that car were in the ignition. I don't know anything else about keys or secret safes. I took half a bottle of whiskey from the glove compartment and—"

Bryce heard the slap. Open palm flesh hitting her cheek.

"Beating me, or any of us, won't change the facts. If there's a lock, can't one of your thugs pick it?"

Bryce inched around the corner.

He had a side view of what was going on. Rosco had father and daughter off to the side. They'd faced the girl against the wall, wearing headphones and playing a game. Her father was taped to a chair next to her. Kylie was leaning against the open car trunk.

He wanted to rush in, guns blazing…okay, gun, he only had one, which wouldn't go far.

Plain and simple…the hostages would be killed.

A confrontation before backup got here…he'd be overpowered, they'd search him, they'd find the drive and he'd be left with no bargaining power.

There was no way to let Kylie know he was there. No way to warn her or the others. Maybe that was Fenley's phone his daughter was playing on. The headphones would keep any notification sound silent. But what if it wasn't?

Rosco turned and opened his palm. Wordlessly, a gun was placed in it. He swiveled and pointed it at Kylie's forehead. Bryce gripped the edge of the corner, ready to spring forward. He'd never get there in time. He raised his Sig and took aim.

KYLIE DIDN'T REMEMBER Daniel Rosco. She searched her memory but couldn't come up with anything. A friend of the Tenorenos or maybe even an enemy. Whoever he was, there was something dead in his eyes that was more frightening than she'd ever experienced.

His gun was about three inches from her eyes. She'd never stared down a gun barrel before. It took a lot of willpower to stand there and not move. One of his men stood next to her ready to keep her in place.

"I don't have it. I don't know what you're talking about," she lied.

"Say I believe you. Someone has checked that car. It's been polished, vacuumed. Who?" Rosco asked, shrugging and dropping the barrel to point at her toes. "Bring him. Take the girl to my car."

Once Darla was outside, he turned the gun toward Grant. She didn't doubt that Rosco would pull the trigger. He inched closer and closer.

"All right. Stop. It's me. I'm the only one that knew about the extra key." She held her hands up as Rosco's gun pointed at her face again. "I hid it under the driver's seat just before I was abducted by those monsters."

Don't antagonize them. She could hear Bryce's voice in her head even though she was certain he'd never said those exact words before. She didn't really have a choice. She couldn't let him hurt Grant or Darla.

"That's closer to the truth. Get the key." Rosco used the barrel as a pointing stick toward the car.

"Mr. Rosco, you want us to check around the building? Make sure everything's secure?" The one who had ridden in the back asked, shifting from foot to foot.

"Stay put. I don't want to draw any attention to this place. No one knows where we are or even *who* we are."

Except Grant, Darla and me.

She took her time, not about to rush anything. The slower she moved the more time Bryce had to find them. She stroked the Cadillac's fin-shaped fender. "So when did we meet, Daniel? It couldn't have been at the Tenoreno Christmas party. They only invited friends to that."

"We were invited, but didn't attend. Xander and I ran into each other at a club opening. He had you draped on his arm."

Kylie took a deep breath seeking a calm place before she opened the passenger door and stretched across the seat to find the key. She knew exactly where it was, but stalled a little and took her time.

"Kylie?" Grant sounded frightened.

She looked over the edge of the car, scooting to her knees. The gun was back against Grant's temple. She held the key up. "I found it."

"Let's get something straight, Sissy. I've had some restless nights recently and I'm ready to head home. No more delays."

She tossed the key at his feet. "What incentive do I have to comply? Aren't you going to kill us anyway?"

"Oh, God, not Darla! You can't—" Grant got a face full of metal for his outburst. He fell to the warehouse floor.

Kylie searched the room for a possible place to run. And that's when she saw Bryce. He'd found them. He signaled to keep stalling. Hopefully that meant there were more officers coming. She had to trust him and get close to Grant so she could let him know. She hurried to her neighbor's side.

"Open the safe, Sissy. Don't play games," Rosco

said, kicking the key toward her. "I know you've already been inside."

He really believed there was no one following his men to this place. "Are you okay, Grant?" She leaned closer, checking his head. He tried to rise, she pushed him back down. "That's a deep cut." She lowered her voice. "Help is here. Stay low and take cover when the rescue happens." Then louder, "Are you okay to sit?"

"I'm just a little woozy."

They worked together, moving him closer to the wheel of the car. He could roll under it or even make it to the semitrailer. It would make it easier on their rescuers if they stayed together.

"Now that you've taken care of your boy-friend—open my safe."

Should she keep up the pretense? She tried not to look toward Bryce, but she did anyway. She wouldn't climb into the back of that car and potentially be caught inside—or even locked inside.

She held up the key and leaned over the edge. She found the keyhole with her fingertip and guided the key inside. Then she felt around for the magnetic hide-a-key, freed it and tossed it to Rosco.

"That's what you wanted. I don't know why I had to retrieve it for you."

"Don't you?" He slid the compartment open and removed a flash drive. It looked close to what he'd put there five years ago.

Kylie prayed that he couldn't remember the differences. "No." But she did. "If you're afraid that I shared the information with the police, the fact that I'm not under their protection is proof that I didn't. They let me go. And getting involved now is the furthest thing from my mind. I haven't plugged it in or looked at any part of it."

"On the other hand, she did give me the real one." Bryce swaggered around the corner like he was walking down Pecan Street trying to get her attention. Hands toward the ceiling, no weapon in sight, no sign of a bulletproof vest...he tossed a flash drive—hopefully not *the* flash drive—in the air. "I don't know what's on that thing you've got, but I do know what's on this."

He stopped when all the guns in the room turned toward him.

"Now, do you think I'd waltz in here without backup?" Bryce tossed the flash drive into the air like a ball, caught it and shoved it in his pocket. "You're done, Rosco. So are your friends, including Xander Tenoreno."

Rosco tipped his head toward his men.

She stood next to a seated Grant urging Bryce to start moving.

Two smoke grenades bounced across the concrete floor, leaving a trail of gray mist in their wake. Bryce darted behind a wooden crate as the guns close to her began firing.

In other words, all hell broke loose.

Chapter Twenty-Three

Chaos. A man ran past him, but that wasn't his objective. The hostages were. There was a plan in place and he had his role. He wasn't physically prepared for the tear gas, although he knew it was coming. Bryce didn't have time to cover his mouth and nose. He held his breath and waited for the cover of smoke before heading to the Cadillac.

Trent shouldn't have fired the gas into the warehouse until they had the little girl out of harm's way. The Dublin police, Fred and Richard were waiting outside to grab the five men helping Rosco. Bryce needed to find Fenley and Kylie.

"Run!" she shouted.

It wasn't to him, so she must be instructing Fenley. He ran toward her voice, toward the door at the loading dock. Someone, severely coughing, staggered through the opening and then down the first couple of steps. Fred was there and lowering his shotgun.

"Grant, where's Kylie?" Fred asked, burying his face in the crook of his elbow.

"He got her. She told me to run. I couldn't see. I came to find Darla—I thought you were still in there to help her." Grant Fenley looked at Bryce with his explanation for leaving Kylie.

"Two men unaccounted for, Bryce!" Fred yelled after him as he re-entered the building.

He instinctively knew that Rosco was the snake who had Kylie. He pulled his shirt over his nose and mouth to avoid the smoke now rising and clearing. Something moved in the direction he'd come through earlier. He followed, gun at the ready.

Bryce approached and rounded the corner he'd hidden behind. No one was there, but he heard something crash. He followed through the front and out the door, ducking back when shots ricocheted off the solid door and hit the glass window.

"Rosco! All I want is Kylie." Bryce couldn't tell where the shots had been fired from. He ducked to the ground and belly-crawled through the door.

He listened, trying to hear anything other than the shouts on the other side of the building. Then he heard it, scuffling, gravel hitting the steps to his right.

Staying low, then smashing himself against the building, he got closer into position. He turned ready to fire. But Rosco had Kylie in front of him, covering his body like the kidnappers had used the little girl.

"Ranger, I swear I'll put a bullet in her brain. I want a car to take me back to my plane. Then..."

Rosco talked. Bryce's gaze met Kylie's. She spread four fingers across Rosco's forearm that held her captive around her neck. Then three. Bryce barely nodded acknowledging that he understood. She was going to do something at the end of the countdown. He just didn't know what.

"Tell me this, Daniel," she said. "Was it you or Xander who shot my friends?"

Rosco's gun was aiming at him, then at Kylie. "You aren't calling for a car, Ranger."

Down to two fingers as the gun moved. Now he had the timing.

"Answer her question." Bryce pulled his phone from his pocket and dialed Fred. "Might as well let her know it was you."

Rosco took small steps back. Bryce couldn't tell if he was dragging Kylie along or if she was forcing him onto the gravel where he could lose his footing. One finger.

Bryce was ready. The gun swung away from him and he moved forward at the same time Kylie bent the fingers around her neck toward his wrist and made Rosco tilt back and away from her.

She fell to the ground, hitting Rosco's knees together.

It didn't work. She stared into eyes that looked

prepared for her attack or defense. But Bryce was there. She flattened herself to the ground, ready to roll out of the way.

Bryce sent a double punch to the man's gut, then another to his jaw. The gun flew. Kylie scrambled to her knees to capture the gun and keep it from Rosco's hands. Bryce took a couple of punches to his body, but sent an uppercut to the other man's jaw. Rosco fell backward hitting the gravel.

Fred came running around the corner. Kylie was in the older man's embrace while Bryce rolled Rosco to his stomach and yanked his arm behind him, pinning him to the ground.

"That didn't look like much of a fight," Fred stated.

"Not much of an opponent. That's what happens when they get arrogant." Kylie sniffed and wiped her eyes from the tear gas.

"Good enough to put bullets in you," Rosco spit into the gravel.

"Want me to take him off your hands?" Fred asked.

They exchanged places and Bryce took Kylie around the corner. The adrenaline wore off and she broke down in his arms for a couple of minutes. Real tears on top of the watering eyes from the tear gas.

"It wasn't Xander. I won't wonder anymore who killed my friends. It's over. Really over."

"Everything except the paperwork." He grinned

at her and gave her a brief kiss. "It's going to get crowded around here with all the law enforcement headed this direction, but I don't want you out of my sight."

"Yes, sir. Ranger, sir." She playfully saluted. "Don't worry, I don't plan to leave your side."

"COME WITH ME." Bryce tugged a little on her elbow to get her moving. The sun was sinking and he wanted to slip away without a lot of questions.

"Don't I need to hang around or be whisked off for a more formal interrogation? I know they're going to accuse me of something else."

He looked over his shoulder to see if anyone was following. "That's what I'm trying to avoid."

"Okay, I was joking, but you clearly aren't. Are they going to accuse me of knowing about that flash drive? You were with me. You know that—"

He spun her around and sealed her lips with his. "You scared me to death, woman. I thought I'd be identifying your dead remains somewhere. Try not to come to anybody's rescue except mine. Will ya?"

Their lips tangled in a deep kiss that would have lasted longer but was interrupted by someone clearing his throat.

"Want me to come back later?"

"Dad!"

"That would be me. Nice to see you again." His father took Kylie's hand between his.

"My dad's taking you to his ranch until most of this blows over. You'll be safe there while I get things straightened out." Bryce wanted to move them along, but he didn't know which direction his dad had come from.

"I'm not going anywhere without you."

"Thing is, if you stay here, you'll probably have to and there won't be anything I can do about it. Trust me on this."

"You're in just as much trouble as me." She crossed her arms and he knew she was stubborn enough to go to jail if need be.

"She has a point, son. I can fly you to Waco tomorrow. Just tell them you'll be back." His dad shrugged like it was no big deal.

"Yeah, tell them you'll be back, Bryce," Kylie echoed.

He could swear he could hear her toe tapping on the road. "What are you driving, Dad?"

"Hickson let me borrow his Chevy at the airport." He pointed to an old brown rust bucket. "Got me here. Should get me back."

"I'll meet you around the corner in ten. If I'm not there…" He gave his father a look that meant he was to take Kylie with him no matter what.

"Be there." She pulled his face toward hers and kissed him. She looped her arm with his dad's and they strolled down the street. "Did you know your son, the big bad Gunslinger, took down the bad guy without firing a shot?"

Bryce wanted to hear the rest of that conversation. Instead, he found Fred and Richard to make arrangements for his truck. He found Major Parker who was inside the warehouse accepting the appreciation of the police chief for loaning a Texas Ranger to his team.

"More than happy to be of service," Parker answered, shaking hands with all around him. When they'd walked away, he turned to Bryce. "You managed to get everybody out of this alive. Good thing I never put your suspension papers through."

"Yes, sir." The surprise probably made him look like a wide-eyed rookie. "We got the flash drive open. It's full of old border crossing maps and has some photographic evidence that the Rosco family was involved in exactly what we thought. You name it, they smuggled it. I think it'll help the state's case against Tenoreno if we can prove they worked together."

"You know you were lucky you came out of this unscathed," his boss said.

"One riot, one ranger. Right, sir?" Bryce hesitated waiting for a shoe or handcuff to drop somewhere. "So I'm going to head out then. See you tomorrow?"

"Why don't you take vacation? I've already called headquarters. They're going to interview Miss Scott next week. Then you won't have to look so guilty about hiding her."

"Yes, sir. That should work out great."

"Yeah, I bet it will." Parker stuck out his hand. "Good job, Bryce. Thanks for keeping our word to the lady."

Bryce shook his major's hand and ran to catch his father and their flight to the Rockin' J.

Chapter Twenty-Four

Less than two hours ago, they'd been involved in an abduction and shoot-out. Kylie had to take a moment to breathe.

Bryce had whisked her off to a private airfield where they'd climbed into his father's tiny airplane. The ride had almost been straight up and straight down, arriving faster than Bryce could explain why they were coming. He didn't really have to. She knew. She needed to be stashed someplace safe until all the hoopla had blown over and the Austin state lawyers decided how important she was or wasn't.

This visit, Bryce's mom was unusually quiet as they entered the house and showed Kylie to the same bedroom she'd slept in before. Instead of following her into the kitchen, she spread out on the bed with a wet cloth across her eyes to help with the stinging from the tear gas. The door opened and Bryce leaned against it.

"Do you really think my ex-husband had nothing to do with this?"

"If he does, we'll find the connection. But my gut tells me that Rosco tried to kill you for his own perverted reasons. Maybe vengeance? Or even to get into Tenoreno's good graces. I think if your ex had any knowledge, Rosco would have brought him down when he bragged about it to us."

"You're probably right."

"You doing okay, Kylie?"

"Honestly, I don't know how I should feel. For five years I've thought Xander hated me enough to kill me." Kylie dropped her arm over her eyes, shutting out the ceiling, the bloodstained gravel and the confession of her friends' murderer.

"There'll be an investigation that might take a while. We have time to find out the truth." He left the door, standing next to the bed. "Hey, my parents turned in early. Let's go stick our feet in the pool."

They left their shoes in the bedroom and silently raced to the pool, sticking their feet in the cool water. She could hear music from across the patio and saw a silhouette of a couple dancing.

"Your parents are cool." She grinned from ear to ear hearing the music of Frankie Valli. "So what's the story on you singing to me?"

"That's a family joke. Strictly need-to-know basis."

She really wanted to know. In fact, she had a

theory and needed to discover the inside story of the person she loved.

Yes, loved.

There it was…she said it—or thought it. There was something about Bryce that she'd fallen in love with from the moment she watched him jerk his shirt over his head and get it caught on his ear.

She hoped it meant he cared for her, but she let it go. "You have a nice family. I'm looking forward to their jokes."

"Good thing, since you'll be staying with them awhile." Bryce splashed the water. It didn't seem to matter that the bottoms of their jeans were getting soaked.

"I don't want to be a bother."

"That will never happen. They'll love the company. You'll be lucky if the entire family's not here within a couple of days. Which means I should probably stick around to protect you from any and all accusations thrown your direction."

"I'm looking forward to getting that family secret out of them, but why would they come?"

"I've never brought anyone home before. Ever. Now I've done it twice in a week. They'll be curious." He reached into the water, splashing it on her face.

Cool. Refreshing. Playfulness. She wanted it all, especially him. "Maybe you can let them know this is for work and head them off."

"Kylie." He tangled his foot with hers, reminding her of when he yanked her into his pool. "If you want this to stay professional, then I need to take you to Company F tomorrow and hand you off to someone else. I want you to be safe, but I didn't bring you here just to protect you."

"What a relief." She laughed and lay back against the tile. "I was hoping this wasn't all one-sided."

The man she'd fallen so fast and so hard for cupped her cheeks with his cool palms. Tilting her head to look past her eyes into her heart.

"Is it too soon to say I love you?" he whispered before devouring her lips.

She wanted to fall into the pool with him and mesh their bodies as close as possible. She almost did just so he could get her out of her clothes, but a look over Bryce's shoulder revealed his parents watching from their patio door.

Wait. The word repeated in her head while she kissed him. But she didn't care if his parents watched. She didn't care that someone else was discovering Rosco's motive or that Xander might have been involved.

Nope. All she cared about was kissing Bryce. She was a little frightened to stop capturing the sweet taste of his mouth. If she stopped, he might answer his own question. Might say it *was* too soon to talk about love. Then again…they'd come so close to losing each other before ever being together.

"Damn, you are so beautiful. Inside and out. I

see my soul tangled with yours when I look into your blue eyes."

"And I see my future in yours. I wouldn't have had one if you hadn't come looking for me. I'm so happy you did."

That was all the encouragement he needed. She wrapped her arms around him and planned to end each of her days there for the rest of her life.

Epilogue

Four years later

Kylie sat under an umbrella on the porch watching Bryce mow the lawn. Four years with him and it still felt strange to go sleeveless and not cover the scars—even if they had been smoothed a bit by surgery. His confidence and effortless love for her is what made it possible.

The spring air was warm and she couldn't wait to get the pool stabilized and running. Fred and Richard had the teens come by for some work. The men taught them how to put in a small fence. Babyproofing the yard for their godchild had been on their minds all winter. Now it was done and Bryce was determined to get everything ready for the barbecue baby shower next weekend.

That is, if they made it to next weekend. The baby kicked and her muscles tightened. "Shush, baby. Those silly Braxton Hicks contractions are getting to me, too." She smoothed her tummy, receiving another kick for her efforts. "You are going to be just as demanding as your daddy."

Even through her sunglasses she could tell he was getting red. It was the first time he'd been in the sun this season. They went through the same thing every year. She waved at her husband and got his attention. "Bryce, hon. Come and let me put sunscreen on your back and shoulders before it's too late."

"I'm nearly done."

"Bryce, come on. I came outside to put this on you and have been waiting. We haven't bought any aloe yet. Don't come to me when you're blistered and suffering. I'm not running to the store at midnight."

He shrugged and continued mowing. He'd done all the yardwork without a shirt and without sunscreen. She'd come out to sit in an uncomfortable chair to spray his back. But when he'd switched lawn tools she had been inside making lemonade. She shifted in the cushioned swivel chair attempting to get comfortable.

It was impossible.

The mower's buzz hushed and Bryce joined her, plopping tiredly into the chair next to her. The false contraction came again with a wallop. The baby was demanding attention, acting crowded.

"This chair was a lot more comfortable when we bought it last year. Or maybe I just fit it better then. Along with my clothes, my shoes…I even think my toothbrush fit better then."

Bryce laughed, then tipped back the lemonade she'd brought out on the same serving tray she'd used when they'd first met. What else could he do but laugh? She was the grouchy one. Even though the false labor had them both on edge, he still grinned at her. Braxton Hicks contractions for weeks. Two practice runs to the hospital had made them both feel like overanxious beginners.

"Ow." She rubbed her belly. "Seriously, I don't know how much more of this I can take."

He set the glass on the tray next to the pitcher. "Probably all of it. You're going to be a great mom."

"You know just what to say."

He leaned forward and talked directly to the baby. "Hey, little man. You're giving your mom a hard time. I think you both need a nap." Then looking up at her. "What do you say? Is it—Wow. Was that a real contraction for once?"

"Just one of those silly Braxton Hicks. They've been coming all day."

"As in every couple of minutes all day?" He looked at his watch.

"No. Or I don't think so. I try to ignore them." Now that she was thinking about it, the pain was a little more in her lower back. "Owwww. Okay, that was pretty close to the other one."

"Too close. How do you feel about having a baby

today?" He didn't sit back. Instead he spread his hands across the baby and kept them there, waiting.

"But it's three weeks earlier than they thought."

"It's not an exact science, Kylie. I think we should go."

"You don't want to call the doctor? Ask an opinion? Wait to see if it's just indigestion?" She smiled at him, trying to get him to smile. He looked too dang serious for either of their sanity. "Come on, Bryce. Both trips to the hospital, they said my water would probably break. That hasn't happened. I don't want to be sent home again."

"Hon, I can do a lot of things, but delivering my own baby is not one of them." He popped up from the chair. "You stay here. I know where everything is."

"Babe, my bag is already in the truck. You put it there two days ago."

"Right. Do you want to change clothes or anything? Should I? I should since I probably stink. Do we have time for that?" He was taking a step toward the house, then back to her and then toward the house.

"Are you okay? You look really nervous." Kylie laughed, ignoring the discomfort.

"I'm, ah…yeah, I'm fine."

"How about a sho—wer. Oh boy, that was rough." She wanted to huff and puff her way through it. "Maybe you're right and we should sort of hurry."

"That was about a minute and a half after the

last one." He helped her to her feet. "Let's go. I'll call the doctor's service on the way."

"Sweetheart, you really do need to change."

"I'll be okay."

"But I won't. I'm not going through six hours of labor with you standing next to me smelling like a wildebeest."

He raised his arm—just like a man—and sniffed. "I guess I do smell sort of rank. I don't want to put this off."

"At least grab some clean clothes, hon. Please? I'll wait for you in the truck."

Bryce took one more sniff and unbuckled his shorts, dropping them on the way to the pool, hopped over the three-foot fence and jumped into the icy water.

Kylie watched, sort of in shock, until another contraction hit. Dripping freezing water, Bryce came back to her at the end and helped her limp to the truck.

"What made you think of a wildebeest?"

"We took the boys to the zoo and there was that awful smell." Kylie leaned on Bryce to get in the truck. No choice there. She wasn't only nine months pregnant, she was also midcontraction.

"That was a skunk, babe."

The contraction was tighter and lower and following more quickly. "Uuuh…just hurry with those clothes."

Then the smell of fried chicken permeated her

nostrils. She looked in the back and sure enough, there was a sack. Bryce had a habit of leaving his lunch bones in the truck so Honeybear couldn't find them in the trash.

The smell in the truck, the pool, the stress, the worry…it all brought back the reminder of how far they'd come in four years. The first time she'd had Bush's chicken she'd been falling a little bit more in love with the man she couldn't live without now.

The Tenoreno family couldn't hurt them anymore. Daniel Rosco had been prosecuted for the murders of her friends. His confession and the evidence on the flash drive sent him to prison for life. He'd taken a video of their bodies as proof he'd completed the job. Then lost the Cadillac in a bet that she would die. She shivered, not wanting to think about it again.

On a happier note, the teen and senior program she'd begun in Hico had an interim director while she'd be home with the baby. And on their last trip for pie, they'd run into the Fenley family. Darla was doing well and had tried to stretch her arms around Kylie's growing baby belly—something Bryce joked about being unable to do all the time.

"We've had such a wonderful life already, baby boy. You are going to make it completely full. Oh…goodness." That contraction felt a little more intense. She leaned her head out the window. "Bryce! Hurry!"

He came barreling under the garage door as it started to close. Shooing Honeybear back underneath with his socks and boots in his hands.

"I'm using the lights."

She grabbed her stomach, breathing hard. "I think you should."

He pushed his hair back out of his eyes, looked through the pile he'd dumped on the seat and found his glasses. Then put the truck in gear. "I love you."

Each time he told her it was special. Each time he made her feel like it was the first time he'd ever admitted that he loved anyone.

"I love you, babe. Now get this truck moving." She squeezed his hand and flipped the flashing lights on herself.

Bryce grinned and ran the first stop sign. "Time for baby Johnson to make his debut."

* * * * *

Don't miss the next book in Angi Morgan's
TEXAS RANGERS: ELITE TROOP
*miniseries when HARD CORE LAW
goes on sale next month.*

*You'll find it wherever
Harlequin Intrigue books
and ebooks are sold!*

LARGER-PRINT BOOKS!

HARLEQUIN

Presents®

PASSION
GUARANTEED
SEDUCTION

GET 2 FREE LARGER-PRINT NOVELS PLUS 2 FREE GIFTS!

YES! Please send me 2 FREE LARGER-PRINT Harlequin Presents® novels and my 2 FREE gifts (gifts are worth about $10). After receiving them, if I don't wish to receive any more books, I can return the shipping statement marked "cancel." If I don't cancel, I will receive 6 brand-new novels every month and be billed just $5.30 per book in the U.S. or $5.74 per book in Canada. That's a saving of at least 12% off the cover price! It's quite a bargain! Shipping and handling is just 50¢ per book in the U.S. and 75¢ per book in Canada.* I understand that accepting the 2 free books and gifts places me under no obligation to buy anything. I can always return a shipment and cancel at any time. Even if I never buy another book, the two free books and gifts are mine to keep forever.

176/376 HDN GHVY

Name	(PLEASE PRINT)	
Address		Apt. #
City	State/Prov.	Zip/Postal Code

Signature (if under 18, a parent or guardian must sign)

Mail to the **Reader Service:**
IN U.S.A.: P.O. Box 1867, Buffalo, NY 14240-1867
IN CANADA: P.O. Box 609, Fort Erie, Ontario L2A 5X3

**Are you a subscriber to Harlequin Presents® books
and want to receive the larger-print edition?
Call 1-800-873-8635 today or visit us at www.ReaderService.com.**

* Terms and prices subject to change without notice. Prices do not include applicable taxes. Sales tax applicable in N.Y. Canadian residents will be charged applicable taxes. Offer not valid in Quebec. This offer is limited to one order per household. Not valid for current subscribers to Harlequin Presents Larger-Print books. All orders subject to credit approval. Credit or debit balances in a customer's account(s) may be offset by any other outstanding balance owed by or to the customer. Please allow 4 to 6 weeks for delivery. Offer available while quantities last.

Your Privacy—The Reader Service is committed to protecting your privacy. Our Privacy Policy is available online at www.ReaderService.com or upon request from the Reader Service.

We make a portion of our mailing list available to reputable third parties that offer products we believe may interest you. If you prefer that we not exchange your name with third parties, or if you wish to clarify or modify your communication preferences, please visit us at www.ReaderService.com/consumerchoice or write to us at Reader Service Preference Service, P.O. Box 9062, Buffalo, NY 14240-9062. Include your complete name and address.

HPLP15

LARGER-PRINT BOOKS!
GET 2 FREE LARGER-PRINT NOVELS PLUS
2 FREE GIFTS!

◆HARLEQUIN®

Romance

From the Heart, For the Heart

YES! Please send me 2 FREE LARGER-PRINT Harlequin® Romance novels and my 2 FREE gifts (gifts are worth about $10). After receiving them, if I don't wish to receive any more books, I can return the shipping statement marked "cancel." If I don't cancel, I will receive 4 brand-new novels every month and be billed just $5.09 per book in the U.S. or $5.49 per book in Canada. That's a savings of at least 15% off the cover price! It's quite a bargain! Shipping and handling is just 50¢ per book in the U.S. and 75¢ per book in Canada.* I understand that accepting the 2 free books and gifts places me under no obligation to buy anything. I can always return a shipment and cancel at any time. Even if I never buy another book, the two free books and gifts are mine to keep forever.

119/319 HDN GHWC

Name	(PLEASE PRINT)

Address	Apt. #

City	State/Prov.	Zip/Postal Code

Signature (if under 18, a parent or guardian must sign)

Mail to the **Reader Service:**
IN U.S.A.: P.O. Box 1867, Buffalo, NY 14240-1867
IN CANADA: P.O. Box 609, Fort Erie, Ontario L2A 5X3
Want to try two free books from another line?
Call 1-800-873-8635 or visit www.ReaderService.com.

* Terms and prices subject to change without notice. Prices do not include applicable taxes. Sales tax applicable in N.Y. Canadian residents will be charged applicable taxes. Offer not valid in Quebec. This offer is limited to one order per household. Not valid for current subscribers to Harlequin Romance Larger-Print books. All orders subject to credit approval. Credit or debit balances in a customer's account(s) may be offset by any other outstanding balance owed by or to the customer. Please allow 4 to 6 weeks for delivery. Offer available while quantities last.

Your Privacy—The Reader Service is committed to protecting your privacy. Our Privacy Policy is available online at www.ReaderService.com or upon request from the Reader Service.

We make a portion of our mailing list available to reputable third parties that offer products we believe may interest you. If you prefer that we not exchange your name with third parties, or if you wish to clarify or modify your communication preferences, please visit us at www.ReaderService.com/consumerschoice or write to us at Reader Service Preference Service, P.O. Box 9062, Buffalo, NY 14240-9062. Include your complete name and address.

HRLP15

LARGER-PRINT BOOKS!
GET 2 FREE LARGER-PRINT NOVELS PLUS
2 FREE GIFTS!

HARLEQUIN®

super romance®

More Story...More Romance

HSRLP15